ANOTHER DAY, ANOTHER DEATH

Bolan went into the garage, demolishing the door and sending fragmentation rounds ahead of the advance into the interior. One silly guy immediately lurched out of a corner and threw up his hands, screeching for quits. Bolan blew that guy clear through the side of the building, then turned his tumblers loose in a sweep on another man with a chopper who was trying to dance and shoot to the same tune. It could not work, of course. A track of .45's split the floor at Bolan's feet—close enough for sure—and kept on climbing the wall as the guy ended the dance on his back, gliding in his own blood.

And now the big chase was on, the Bolan Watch had gone down—and very soon every cop in North Georgia would be gunning for Mack Bolan's hide. It was a familiar pattern but no less a disturbing one. He'd shaken them before, sure, but he was a realist enough to know that he could not shake them forever. One of these days, a bullet from the same side was going to find *his* blood; that was certain. This could be the day . . .

The Executioner Series:

the EXECUTIONER #27

DIXIE CONVOY

by Don Pendleton

PINNACLE BOOKS   NEW YORK CITY

This is a work of fiction. All the characters and events portrayed in this book are fictional, and any resemblance to real people or incidents is purely coincidental.

EXECUTIONER #27: DIXIE CONVOY

Copyright © 1976 by Pinnacle Books, Inc.

An original Pinnacle Books edition, published for the first time anywhere.

ISBN: 0-523-00947-X

First printing, December 1976

Cover illustration by Gil Cohen

Printed in the United States of America

PINNACLE BOOKS, INC.
275 Madison Avenue
New York, N.Y. 10016

For the road buddies, everywhere:
the good numbers are on you.
It's Magnum 44, KGJ1024, on the
side and standing by for a shout.
Bring it on back.

*The last temptation is the
greatest treason;
To do the right deed
for the wrong reason.*
     —T. S. ELIOT

*Let us have faith that right
makes right, and in that faith
let us to the end dare to do our
duty as we understand it.*
     —ABRAHAM LINCOLN

*Right and wrong can be argued
forever, from many viewpoints.
I'm not here for arguments.
I am Judgment, and I have come
for their blood. Drown me in it,
if you must, but tell the world
that Mack Bolan died in the line of duty.*
     —MACK BOLAN, THE EXECUTIONER

TABLE OF CONTENTS

Dixie Convoy

Prologue

This terrain was crowded with ghosts—and Mack Bolan could feel their presence even if he could not see them.

It was hallowed ground.

Many thousands of gallant warriors had lent their lifeblood to the fertility of this soil.

Worst of all, the dead of all these armies had been, in reality and in their deaths, "soldiers of the same side."

Yeah, and the ghosts still maneuvered along that fateful corridor between Chattanooga and Atlanta. Swirling little gusts of rustling wind whispered of Chickamauga, Missionary Ridge and Orchard Knob, Lookout Mountain, Peachtree Creek, and other combat arenas, where grim and desperate armies had clashed and bled and lent sanctity to madness. Creeping kudzu vines interlaced the

1

forests and wove their magic web to the sun as though fueled in their search (and in their union) by the myriad streams of human blood that had once soaked this corridor of insanity.

And, sure, Mack Bolan could understand the vibrations of this place. His was a kindred spirit, and warfare was something he had come to understand long ago. Battlefields changed, sure—tactics evolved and weaponry improved—but the basic ingredient of all warfare remained pretty much the same. It all boiled down, finally, to a contest between gladiators. The spirit of the gladiator had probably changed very little since the dawn of man. And, yes, Bolan could certainly empathize with that spirit. He could understand the fear, the despair, the weariness, the anger, and the agony. He had experienced it all. He was, indeed, experiencing it now.

Forget the sides and forget the causes; Sherman, Bragg, Rosecrans, Thomas, Johnston—not to mention a couple of hundred thousand nameless others—had fought the good fight here, in this place, at a time far removed. Their reasons were probably no more and no less noble than any gladiator's at any time or place. Warriors did not supply the reasons, merely the means. Their only goal was victory; their only hope, survival.

Men did not *make* wars. They simply fought them.

Wars were made somewhere else—maybe even in some other world—by the fates, perhaps, or by the gods of human destiny. Or maybe they were built into the evolutional structure of the universe. Bolan had never pretended to understand the *whys* of warfare—only the *ways*.

2

No man had ever died in combat who truly understood why he must be there and why he must kill and be killed. The effective gladiator did not cloud his mind with such abstracts. He simply stood and fought, with all his mind and heart and body. The universe itself took care of the rest.

So, no—Mack Bolan did not question why he was here, on this haunted battlefield between Chattanooga and Atlanta. He asked neither why he must kill nor *if* he must kill. He *knew* the *ways* of warfare. And he knew what must be done.

The grim-eyed warrior final-checked his weapons. Then he mentally tipped his hat to the Blue Ghosts and to the Gray Ghosts as he muttered to the wind: "Here we go again, guy."

hard, probing. "The answer won't affect our friends

1: A Time for War

He was dressed in black, and his hands and face had been treated with a black cosmetic. At the right hip on military web rode the big silver autoloading .44 Magnum. A black 9-mm. "quiet piece"—a Beretta Brigadier with specially engineered silencer—was in shoulder leather at his left chest. Utility belts crossed the torso, from which dangled an assortment of small grenades and other choice items of ordnance—all meticulously selected and "touch-placed" on the belts for instant access. Spare clips for the pistols girded the waist. Slit pockets at the legs carried useful accessories. A leather holster clipped to the web belt in front held a compact walkie-talkie with Citizens Band capability. Slung across the back of the shoulders in a horizontal carry was the M-16/M-79 combo, the "big-punch capability." The M-16 combat rifle would spit a withering stream of 5.56-mm. tumblers at the rate of 700 rounds per minute. She rode atop the M-79, a breech-loading 40-mm. cannon that could hurl high explosive, shot, smoke, or gas rounds.

Although he was already loaded like an army mule, he then selected two "Buck Rogers bazookas"—the Light Anti-tank Weapon, or LAW—armor-piercing missiles that came packed in their own throwaway launchers. He hefted the fiber-glass tubes to his shoulder and struck off cross-country on foot, leaving the scout car parked in the greenery beside the access road.

The time was precisely midnight when he gained the low knoll that had been selected as fire base for this mission. The moon was playing tag with fractured puffs of low cumulus scudding over the mountains to the north, providing an on/off lighting effect upon the terrain.

The Southern skies were reflecting the far-off lights of the queen city, Atlanta, about twenty miles downcountry. At his left hand, Marietta slumbered quietly; at his right, the dark shadow of Kennesaw Mountain rose into the night. Directly ahead, in a cluster of muted lights, lay the target—a collection of warehouses and service buildings, at a range of about five hundred meters.

It looked innocent enough, much like any other trucking terminal: small cluster of warehouses, service garage, small office building, scales house, a few other incidental buildings. The main difference here was the high chain link fence topped with barbed wire, the manned gatehouse, uniformed security patrols.

But Bolan had been in there twice already—once

in a casual daylight recon from the cab of a truck and again in a quiet nighttime infiltration for a prolonged scouting mission.

And, yeah, he had their numbers.

The "security guards" were genuine Mafia hard men, captained by one Thomas Lago, *née* Lagossini, an old hardhead from the New York wars. The full force numbered twenty men, with the normal shift staffing no more than three guns, beefed up to six to eight during critical operations.

The management was pure civilian—dumb men. Perhaps the manager himself, a guy named Harrison, knew what was really moving through those warehouses; the other employees would be kept dumb.

Bolan, also, knew what was moving through those warehouses: contraband of several varieties, including drugs, guns, untaxed cigarettes, and whiskey.

This one was the "hard point." Other terminals in the area operated much more openly, dealing chiefly in general merchandise such as television sets, kitchen appliances, and so forth—all stolen from various regions of the country and funneled through the Dixie Corridor for transshipment elsewhere. In addition, the largest stolen-car "recycle" operated from this area.

It was big business, tapping the already weakened American economy to the tune of several billions of dollars a year. Very easy money for the mob, yeah, and several new Mafia empires had been built beneath the cover of this operation.

Bolan's entrance into the corridor had been via Mexico, along the heroin trail. The Atlanta area had become one of the chief U.S. "dumps" for the white powder from Mexico. There were powder factories all over town, where the stuff was cut and packaged for reshipment to the various wholesale markets around the country. This "terminal" served the heroin trail like a revolving door, receiving the raw stuff from Mexico and then distributing the finished product to the street outlets.

But no more.

Bolan's timing was perfect, straight on the numbers.

A truck convoy was just then beginning to move away from the warehouse complex. Six big eighteen-wheelers were moving in close formation just outside the gate and pulling toward the access road. This would be the guns shipment for Ireland, disguised as farm machinery, moving via the Port of Savannah. Bolan had those numbers, too.

The drivers of those trucks were dumb men also; special provisions had been made for that in the mission planning. He gave them half the distance to the road; then he thumbed an HE round into the sliding breech of the M-79 and lofted it onto the roadway a hundred feet in front of the convoy, following immediately with another round to the rear. Scarcely a heartbeat separated the two explosions. The line of trucks stumbled to an immediate halt.

"Cotton *picker*!" came an exclamation through the radio. "What's that up there at the front door?"

Another excited voice rode the airwaves to announce: "Whatever it is, we got one at the back door, too!"

Bolan coolly told them what it was. "You're bracketed, cotton pickers. Bail out and beat it, over the hill and far away. The first wheel to roll gets one dead center."

An intensification of personal risk, sure. Bolan knew that the police routinely monitor the truckers' CB channel. In these hills, CB range could be spotty and unsure; still, a savvy cop could tumble to something going down in the area—or, at worst, the truckers could put out a Ten-thirty-four, a call for help, and pinpoint the location. But it was a necessary gamble. Mack Bolan did not make war on civilians.

The immediate reaction to his challenge, though, was a shocked, "Mercy goodness!" It was a substitute expletive favored for CB radio use.

A less excited guy announced, "We definitely got a problem here, good buddies."

Bolan assured one and all: "You definitely got that. You're hauling contraband. You've got thirty seconds to gather your gear and clear the fire zone."

"Comb your hair and brush your teeth, boys," suggested a third radio voice from the convoy. It was CB-ese for a police radar unit "taking pictures." In this context, close enough.

The cool, troubled voice was wondering, "How about if we just drop the loads and run on naked? We own these tractors, Mr. Smoky. Impound them, and we're out of business."

"I'm not a Smoky," Bolan told him. "And I'm not impounding; I'm burning. How long will it take to drop the trailers?"

"Not long," was the immediate reply.

"Okay, do it. Is your base on this channel?"

"Try fourteen," the guy replied. "The good numbers on you, sir, whatever you are."

Bolan smiled grimly at that pleasant response as he tuned down to Channel fourteen. "How about you there, Bluebird Base?" he called.

Instantly, came the reply: "Yeah. What the hell is going on out there?"

"You're next. Sound the alarm and get all the civilians out. I want no innocent blood."

"Come back? Come back on that? Who've I got there?"

"You've got hell afoot, buddy. Now do it. You've got sixty seconds."

The cool trucker had also switched channels. He came into it with: "Better do as he says, Ned. They've got artillery or something out here. Better take him seriously."

The base station replied with a weak, "Ten-four."

Immediately, the fire alarms inside the compound began their clamor. Another risk factor, sure—those alarms were probably tied directly to the nearest fire station. But there were a dozen or more civilians in those buildings. And, yeah, the risk was part of the game.

Bolan passed a final instruction in there. "Keep clear of the guards. Those guys are targets. Get your people together and run like hell to the rear. Keep to the rear fence line, and you'll be okay. Ten-four?"

"Ten-four, thanks," came back quickly. "We down. We gone."

The trucker mildly inquired, "What're you going to do, guy?"

"I'm going to shake their house down, guy," Bolan told him.

"Yeah—Ten-four on that. Hey, who've I got here? I think I—what's your handle?"

"Depends on who's calling it," Bolan replied amiably. His eyes were measuring the passage of time. "Hadn't you better be losing that load?"

"It's lost. I'm first man out. Can you eyeball me?"

"I've got you, yeah," Bolan said. "Been good modulating with you, guy. B'bye."

"Hey, wait! You've got the one Georgia Cowboy. Catch you on the flip-flop some day?"

"Probably not, but I'll be looking. Better ball it now, guy. Hammer down."

"Ten-four on that balling it, hammer down. But let me try one time." The guy had a bee in his bonnet, and he just had to get it out. "Would this be the one Big B—the Hellfire Kid?"

Bolan was smiling soberly as he replied, "I guess it might fit. I'm down and gone."

So was the time, he reflected, as he turned off the radio. All the numbers had come together. Six trailers loaded with contraband were lined up neatly just outside the compound. All of the tractors had reached the high ground—except for the "Georgia Cowboy" who seemed to be straggling a bit. The terminal lighting had gone to full bright, and Bolan could see a dozen or so figures hurrying toward the rear. The alarms were still sounding. The gatehouse guard had come outside and was pacing nervously at the gate with a shotgun at his chest. Two other guys in uniform were running in from the perimeter, guns drawn.

Bolan's attention was centered on the "flop house"—a ten-by-fifty-foot mobile home that was parked behind the office. A full backup crew of

11

off-duty hard men usually rested there. And, yeah, they were beginning to straggle outside. He counted three of them in various stages of undress, but each was toting a heavy weapon—automatics, probably.

So okay.

The warning shots had been fired and non-combatants cleared from the fire zone. The numbers were all in and the big clock was reading *go*.

It was a time for war.

"We gone, b'bye," Bolan muttered as he turned to his weapons.

2: The Good Numbers

The first LAW flashed from the tube and rustled angrily through the night toward its rendezvous with the rear trailer, impacting dead center with a flash and a roar to stagger the heavens. Some fifty yards down range, the guy at the gate reflexively hit the deck and rolled for cover behind the small gatehouse. Almost instantly, a secondary explosion snuffed out the first with a whoofing fireball that lit the night and rained burning debris throughout the target zone. And, yeah—bet your best numbers, good buddy—there'd been more than *guns* in that shipment. From the sound and sight of that spectacular secondary, there'd been some heavy explosives as well. And now they were pummeling the night, trumpeting out with horizontal jets to engulf the other trailers in successive fireballs and rippling the earth beneath Bolan's feet.

It was quite a bit better than he'd expected. He

had simply wanted to give those hard men something upfront to think about. But now they were in a pell-mell rout to the rear, and this gave Bolan something to think about. He sent the next LAW into the liquor warehouse, again finding volatile substance and brilliant secondary reactions. Ten thousand cases of good Tennessee whiskey joined the festivities with blue flames and searing heat, sending the reeling hard force in panicky retreat to another quarter.

Bolan left his fire base behind him, closing in on foot and advancing with the M-79 at continual bellow. A well-placed round of HE provided enough slope to a section of the fencing to enable him to walk right up it. He poised there for a moment to send a clip of 5.56 tumblers in a tight wreath around the shoulders of a startled mafioso in khaki uniform who'd come dashing around the corner of the office building for a look-see. The dying blast from the guy's shotgun tore a hole through the wall of the building, but the man himself went down without a murmur.

Two other guys ran out from behind a row of warehouses, gawked at the black-clad figure atop the fence, then hastily reversed course, and quickly disappeared from view without firing a shot. Bolan sent a round of high explosive after them, just to keep them moving, and he went the other way.

Someone up there in the night was screaming, "It's him! It's that Bolan guy! I seen 'im, black suit and all! It's him!"

Another guy yelled, "Shut up, just shut up! Alla you boys, close on me. Pete! You get it up to the hot line and pass the word! Tell 'em this bastard is running crazy out here!"

It was probably "Pete" who yelled back, "Fuck that! I'm planted and I'm staying! It's no good, Tommy. Get a defensive position and hold it! That's the best we can do!"

An angered retort bounced back from somewhere in the cluster of buildings, but the mad din of the moment plus Bolan's own movements reduced the argument to a mere whisper. He had heard and seen enough, though, to know that there was no heart in that army. Against a weak or disadvantaged enemy, it would be a different story entirely; they'd be tough as hell, then. Against an equal force, this outfit did not usually stand well. Bolan had not come for them anyway, and there was no time calculated into his mission planning to allow him to track them down nor did he even desire to.

He went on with the shelling and the burning, making certain that no corner remained untouched. The numbers were moving swiftly now; soon, they would run out completely. Soon, too, the law would be making the scene—and that was always Bolan's cue for a quick and quiet exit. He took no chances on a direct confrontation with the law, those "soldiers of the same side." Most of those soldiers did not know, or did not choose to believe, that Mack Bolan was their brother. From sea to shining sea, in fact, the official orders regarding Mack Bolan were: "shoot on sight!—shoot to kill!" Which was precisely as Bolan preferred it. He'd asked for no license to wage war, nor did he expect one. If the law could get to him, okay. He'd accept that. In the meantime, he would evade them in every way possible short of a shoot-out.

And, yeah, he could hear them coming now,

even above the madness of that fire zone. The trailers were all belching and sizzling; the various warehouses were roaring with abandon and spreading their heat to adjacent buildings which, in turn, were joining the wild dance to oblivion. An inferno, yeah, and there would be no stopping it now until the final ember was spent.

The mission was a complete success. It was time to disengage, to put that place behind him and leave it to the law. But something was drawing him onward, deeper into the inferno, some dumb instinct that gave no heed to numbers and tactical decisions.

Bolan found the source of the summons in a small building deep within the complex of burning warehouses, behind a heavy wooden door implanted solidly into the corrugated metal of the building. He blew the lock away with a thundering round from the AutoMag and pushed his way inside.

His nose knew it first, leaping to an awareness of the situation in there even before the pencil beam from his light illuminated the scene in that hell room. A guy was there—or something that had once been a guy—naked and trussed like a holiday turkey and bearing harsh evidence of the programmed indignities inflicted upon that pitiful flesh.

Bolan steeled himself and reached into the mess in search of a life sign, hoping there would be none. There was not, and he sighed with relief, remembering from the back porch of hell why he hated the Mafia so. He found trousers draped over a chair in the corner of the room along with a wallet, a jackknife, thirty-seven cents in coins. Then he went out of there and flipped up a fresh belt of loads for the M-79, a new mission goal flailing at his nervous system, tracking surely along the line of flaming buildings until he could feel the stink of vermin sifting through his pores.

They were inside the service garage—a defensible position no doubt under ordinary circumstances.

At the moment, Mack Bolan was feeling a bit extraordinary.

He went right in, demolishing the door with HE and sending fragmentation rounds ahead of the advance into the interior. One silly guy immediately lurched out of a corner and threw up his hands, screeching for quits. Bolan blew that silly guy clear through the side of the building, then turned his tumblers loose in a sweep on another guy with a chopper who was trying to dance and shoot to the same tune. It could not work, of course. A track of .45's split the floor at Bolan's feet—close enough, for sure—and kept on climbing up the wall as the guy ended the dance on his back, gliding in his own blood.

Two more had apparently caught some of the frag from Bolan's entry; they were writhing on the floor and calling for help. He sent them his greatest blessing, via the booming AutoMag, then whirled deeper into the darkness of the place in search of more.

A pistol yelped and flamed back there in the black—from floor level, it seemed—then another, close alongside the first but *lower*. A grease pit, sure. Bolan freed a grenade from his ready belt, armed it, and rolled it over. He heard it hit the bottom of the pit and then the sudden cries of consternation from two scrambling hard men; but he was half-way to the door with that place already freed from his mind when the explosion came. He went on without a backward look and kept moving until he was clear of the heat zone. Then Bolan paused for a quick assessment of his situation.

The whole place was in flames. A line of fire trucks was pounding along the access road. A smaller vehicle and two police units could be seen in the close background just behind the burning trailers.

All of which left very little to wonder about, concerning Bolan's "situation."

He'd spent the numbers foolishly, to no practical purpose whatever, and now his line of retreat was blocked. He went on to the south perimeter, blew out another section of fence, and walked toward darkness.

It was going to be a hell of a long march to somewhere. And when those civilians back there began telling their stories to the cops, and when those cops began putting the stories together—well, yeah, maybe there wouldn't be time enough left in Mack Bolan's world to finish that march.

The big-punch combo was once again slung horizontally across the back of his shoulders. He was climbing a gentle slope in light vegetation when the sirens began wailing again, distant sirens, coming in from what seemed every point of the compass. So okay, they'd put it together. And the big chase was on, the Bolan Watch had gone down—and very quickly now every cop in North Georgia would be gunning for Mack Bolan's hide. It was a familiar pattern but no less a disturbing one. He'd shaken them before, sure, but he was a realist enough to know that he could not shake them forever. One of these days, a bullet from the same side was going to find his blood; that was certain.

This could be the day.

And, suddenly, it did not really matter to this wearied man in combat black. He halted, lit a cigarette, and turned back for a parting look along the back track. He'd come no more than a mile. He could no longer see the terminal site, but the skies down there were still very red.

"To hell with it," he muttered to the night.

So he'd blown it all for the sake of a dead turkey. So what did any of it mean, anyway? If a guy couldn't follow his quivers through this curious world what *could* he follow? So the dead had called him, and he'd responded.

So—were the dead all that different from the living?

Bolan smoked the cigarette to a stub, watching the redness in the sky below which a miserable wraith had summoned him to the end of his numbers. And what was it the trucker had said to him, on the radio? "The good numbers on you, sir?"

Yeah. Wrong kind of numbers, though. The CB people referred to the numbers of a long-forgotten fraternity, the Morse telegraphers, and their highly abbreviated courtesies via the Morse wire. Best wishes, love and kisses, that sort of stuff. Bolan's numbers were heartbeats, ticks of a mental clock that told him when it was time to hit and time to git.

He'd been following the wrong numbers this night.

"Hell with it," he muttered again as he dropped the cigarette and turned once again to his route of withdrawal. He was nearing the top of the slope when a soft movement somewhere ahead froze him to his track. The moon was temporarily obscured by a passing cloud, and he was in fair cover with dogwoods and hillside shrubs grouped about him. His hand had gone instinctively to the AutoMag, and the big piece was hanging out there in combat stance before he could intellectually assess the situation. He then put the big piece back to leather, holding his ground quietly and waiting for another sound of the night. Whatever was up there at the top of that ridge would not be a legitimate target for the Executioner's guns.

He waited and watched, willing his eyes to pierce the darkness even while knowing that they would not. Then a dislodged stone began sliding toward him. A sharp intake of breath into laboring lungs told him that *some*one was up there, and close by.

Then suddenly the moon was back and bathing that hillside with its soft light. A figure moved into full relief above Bolan, accompanied by a muffled and probably involuntary exclamation: "Good Lord!"

That face was close and clear, a good face but aghast with its discovery, startled and frightened and triumphant all at once.

"The mere sight of you is enough to scare a man dead," the guy told Bolan in a calm but shaken voice.

A vaguely familiar voice, yeah.

Bolan quietly inquired, "Would that be the Georgia Cowboy?"

"You got 'im," the guy replied. "Glad I found you. You're in bad trouble, Big B. There's a cop in every bush. Come on, I think I can get you out of here. I left my rig up on a farm road, about two minutes from here."

Bolan had not moved a muscle, except those of his jaw. Now he relaxed somewhat, took a thoughtful stance, and told the guy: "You're in bad company, cowboy—dangerous company. It could get you nothing better than a hole in the head."

"One good number deserves another, doesn't it?" the guy said softly.

"You owe me nothing," Bolan replied.

"Maybe I owe you more than you realize. Are you coming or aren't you? We haven't much time."

The Bolan gaze flashed a sudden warmth. "Okay, let's go," he said quietly.

The guy turned and went back up the hill. Bolan followed, without a quiver of adverse instinct.

Curious, sure. But who could say in this curious world? Maybe he'd been following the right numbers all night after all. Or maybe sympathetic ghosts were simply restocking an infinite bag of options on this hallowed ground. Bolan shivered involuntarily and went on. A guy had to have something to believe in. Right now, this gladiator was betting on the good numbers ... whatever their source.

3: Hellbound

The guy's name was Grover Reynolds, age somewhere around the thirty-year mark, bright and likable—and he obviously had a story to tell but did not quite know how to get into it. As it happened, he was also something of a Civil War buff and knew this particular territory like the palm of his hand.

Bolan himself was not a particularly talkative type, especially at a time such as this. The cab of that "naked" tractor was therefore subject to long periods of silence—which suited Bolan fine but which obviously made the other guy a bit uncomfortable. He would cover it by pointing out landmarks as they labored along the dirt tracks of the backcountry in that lights-out run to safe ground.

"That low ridge over there. That's where Sherman wheeled his right flank for the assault on Kennesaw."

"Oh. Uh-huh."

"I thought you'd find that interesting."

"I do."

Several silent moments later: "That's where he started the assault. Shouldn't have. Cost him twenty-five hundred casualties, including Fighting Dan McCook."

Bolan was moved to ask, "Who won the battle?"

"Nobody, really. Johnston withdrew toward Atlanta. Sherman caught him with his pants down at the Chattahoochee, outflanked him, and crossed the river behind him. Hell, Sherman had three armies. I guess you could call it a victory for Joe Johnston just for keeping the guy out of Atlanta as long as he did. He led him a merry damned chase, tell you that. They played chess with each other all through these Georgia hills from early May through the summer. Then, hell, it was—uh, you don't really give a damn about any of this, do you?"

"Any other time, cowboy, yeah, I'd love to hear about it. Right now ... well, right now I guess I'm wondering how you knew where to find me."

"Nothing mysterious about it," the guy assured him. "Like I said, this is my home twenty. Boy and man, I've lived here all my life, except for a couple years in 'Nam and until I decided to get rich on the road."

"You don't sound overjoyed with either experience," Bolan commented quietly.

"No reason to be. We lost at 'Nam, and I've been losing ever since. I don't know, sometimes I wonder what it's all about."

"When you find out, tell me," Bolan muttered. "But right now, tell me how you found me."

"It's so easy, I'm ashamed to tell you." The guy chuckled. "I'd rather you think I'm a genius. But naw, I saw the Smokies tearing up the superslab to get down there, and I saw the damn fire wagons and all the hoop-te-do. I figured they'd bottle you up in that valley. So I circled around and hit the dirt track. I know this country, Big B. I put myself in your place. I knew where you'd break for. But I swear you scared a year's growth out of me. You were a lot faster and a lot more invisible than I'd expected. Hell, I had just gotten there and was looking for a good lookout point when I walked right into your face."

"It was a nice piece of work," Bolan complimented him. "Glad you're not a cop."

"Used to be."

Bolan raised his eyebrows at that. "Yeah?"

The Georgia Cowboy grinned and gave his passenger a cheerful wink. "Yeah. Cobb County deputy. It's a good force."

"So why aren't you still with it?"

"Went to war," Reynolds replied, sobering suddenly. "When I got back, I'd had a belly full of it. Went to farming for a while. Went broke, too, damn quick. I cashed out with enough to buy my first rig—halves, anyway. I've got a partner."

Bolan observed, "Won't support two, though."

"Won't support one, get right down to it. My partner is—well, Shorty's almost a brother, we're that close. We get along fine. We usually wheel it together, one at the pedal and the other in the bunk. Spell each other on the long hauls, you know. Make more hauls that way with the same basic investment. Did you know it costs close to five thousand a year just for road taxes and permits? Time we pay insurance and maintenance costs, we don't see a penny of the first ten thousand. So we went to contract hauls. We—"

"Where's your partner now?"

"Well, uh ... I've been trying to get around to that."

"What's so hard?"

"I don't want you to think that I'm trading numbers with you. You know? I mean, yeah, I've got this problem definitely, but it's not why I came looking for you. Not the only reason."

"Okay," Bolan said, eyeing the guy closely, "we've got that covered. So what's the problem?"

"Like I said, we usually run together. Couple times a month, each of us takes a loner—you know, to give the other some time at home. Short runs we always take alone. Well, I wasn't supposed to have this run tonight. Shorty had this one. Hell, it was just a quickie to Savannah, and I was all set for a night at the home twenty. Then, at ten-thirty, the dispatcher calls and says the load is ready for the scales, the tractor is there, but where the hell is the driver? Nowhere, that's where. And that's just not like Shorty. He's a very responsible guy. I thought at first maybe it could be this new beaver, but then I—"

"What's a beaver?"

"Oh, I use the damn radio so much, I guess I—a woman, you know, a lady breaker."

"Sounds like a putdown," Bolan commented.

"It's not meant to be. And this one really is a beaver—I mean, you know, a lady breaker."

It was a different world, yeah, this CB clutch. A

"breaker," Bolan understood, was a term for anyone using a CB channel.

Reynolds was continuing the explanation and obviously still having a tough time getting into his "problem."

"That's how Shorty met her in the first place. She's, uh, a little weird, I think. College-kid type, but I guess maybe twenty-two or twenty-three years on her, flies around in a red superskate and—"

"What's that?"

"Sports car, sorry. I guess it's a Corvette. I don't know these cars one from another. Well, she has ears on that skate, and I guess she enjoys shaking up the gear grinders on the superslab between Atlanta and Marietta. Runs back and forth, modulating with them in those bedroom tones, you know what I mean, driving the damn guys right up the walls of their cabs. And sometimes she even pulls alongside and flashes at them. You know?"

Bolan supposed that he knew. But he asked, "Flashes what?"

The guy grinned and shrugged. "Whatever's handiest and inspiring, I guess. Sometimes it's topless, sometimes bottomless. Shorty swore that she pulled up beside him once in broad daylight without a damn stitch of anything on. Can you imagine? In a convertible, with the top down?"

"Sounds like great fun," Bolan said. "How many trucks do you lose between Atlanta and Marietta?"

"Don't think there haven't been some close calls."

"You were telling me about Shorty," Bolan reminded him.

"I still am. He comes running in one night, all in a lather. He has actually *met* Miss Superskate of

I-75, see. Claims she followed him right into the terminal, see, and—"

"Bluebird?"

"Yeah, same place. We've been running a contract with them since last year. Hell, I didn't know they were dirty. Well, anyway, Shorty and Miss Superskate have really been getting it on for the past few months. I mean very heavy, see. She's been riding the bunk boards with him on his loner hauls, and I guess he's been riding *her* bunkboards during *my* loners. I don't know for sure about that. Shorty clammed up on the subject of Miss Superskate right damned quick. Got very sensitive about the subject and even had a couple of brawls with our road buddies over her. You know how guys jaw about something like that."

"I don't know where the hell you're taking me, cowboy."

"We'll come out above Kennesaw on Highway 41. From there, you—"

"I was talking about your partner."

"Oh. Well, I don't know how else to tell it. I was working it through my own mind, I guess, trying to figure something logical about tonight. It's not like Shorty to flat not show up for a haul. I called all around for him. I even went through his stuff and found the superskate's phone number. And that's when the whole thing turned definitely strange, I mean definitely for sure. It's his turn for the loner— right? He's been taking her along as his bunkie on the loners—right? So I figured—hell, I don't know what I figured. Except that something is screwy as hell."

"You, uh, are trying to tie it to what happened down there tonight."

"In a way, yeah. See, at first it was just a question of Shorty and the beaver. That was screwy enough. Then when you hit me with this *contraband* rap—well, hell, now I'm really starting to wonder."

"It's the cop in you," Bolan suggested.

"There's not much of that left in me," the guy said, smiling wanly at his passenger. "Bolan ... I'm worried. I'm afraid Shorty has got mixed up in that rat pack."

"Why do you think that?"

"Does the name Sciaparelli mean anything to you?"

Bolan raised a solemn gaze to the guy as he replied, "You bet it does. He's the silent man behind Bluebird. How'd you know?"

Reynolds sighed heavily and lit a cigarette. Presently, he replied, "Call it a hunch. I didn't know for sure until you just now confirmed it."

"Where'd the hunch come from?"

"It came from Miss Superskate's telephone number. I called there, you know, looking for him. A guy answers. He says it's Sciaparelli's residence. It confused me. The beaver's name is supposed to be Rossiter—Jennifer Rossiter. I thought maybe I was blundering into something. You know, an unfaithful wife routine or something. I told the guy I had the wrong number. Then I went on out to the terminal and took the haul myself. Then you hit me with your little bombshell. And that's when I started hunching and worrying. Look, let's put it out flat. I'm not asking for anything except that you'll consider the circumstances. When you go gunning your next round at these guys, if your gunsights happen to fall on my little partner, try to remember what a dazzling beaver can do to a guy to screw him up. All I'm saying is—"

"I know what you're saying," Bolan quietly interrupted, "but I think maybe you're on the wrong tack."

"I hope so. Good Lord, I hope so."

"It could be worse than that, though."

"How could it be worse?"

Bolan quietly handed over to the Georgia Cowboy a wallet, a jackknife, and thirty-seven cents in coins. "It could be this bad," he said.

The tractor lugged to a halt and coughed dead as Reynolds examined the remains of a miserable wraith who had summoned Mack Bolan to his torture/death chamber.

"Where'd you get this?" Reynolds whispered.

"It's his, eh?"

"Yes. Where'd you get it?"

"From the back porch of hell," Bolan told him. "Your partner is dead, and damned glad to be that way, believe it. Don't ask me any more until you're ready to challenge hell. I mean that, cowboy. Don't ask."

The cowboy did not ask. The look in Bolan's eyes was tale enough, for the moment. He started the engine and resumed the silent journey.

Not until the lights of civilization were reflecting on the windshield did the silence break, and then it was Bolan who broke it.

"I'll help you set it straight if that's what you want," he told the guy.

"Yeah. Thanks. That's exactly what I want. Where do we go from here?"

The guy was ready to challenge hell.

"Welcome to the club," Bolan told him soberly.

"Let's go to Acworth. I have a base camp on the lake."

There were, he knew, many routes to hell.

And, yeah, Bolan knew every one of them—like the palm of his hand.

4: Challenged

Bolan took the distraught trucker to his rented cabin on Allatoona Lake, put some coffee on the stove, and washed away the stench of warfare with a quick shower. The coffee was finished when he was, and Reynolds was mechanically going through the motions of filling the cups when Bolan emerged from the bath.

"You look great," the guy grumbled, giving his host a half-interested inspection. "How do you do it?"

"It's a state of mind," Bolan told him. "You'd better start working on yours."

"Guess I'm still a bit stunned."

"That's a state of mind, too," Bolan pointed out.

"Guess you're right." The guy tried a smile, lit a cigarette, tasted the coffee. "You make it right," he commented. "You could get a job in a truck stop."

"Don't get glad, cowboy. Get mad."

"Don't let the smile fool you, soldier. I'm mad as hell."

"Stay that way then. It'll take a lot of it if you intend to hear about your partner."

"I've got plenty of it."

Bolan put on some comfortable clothing, sat down at the table with his coffee, and told the guy all about the final hours of Shorty Wilkins. He did not spare the details. When it was finished, Reynolds went to the toilet and puked. He was in there a long while and came out looking worse than when he went in.

"Still mad?" Bolan quietly asked him.

"No," the cowboy replied weakly, "just sick."

"When the sick goes, you'll be mad again. But the sick will always be there, poised at the back of the mind, ready to leap out at an unsuspecting moment. You'll have trouble eating meat for a while. You'll have more bad dreams than good ones for a long time. And it came to you secondhand—remember that."

Reynolds groaned and stared at his hands. "How do you do it?" he asked weakly.

"How do I do what?"

"How do you keep . . . going on . . . like this?"

"I stay mad."

"I see."

"How you doing?" Bolan asked gruffly.

"I'll make it." The guy lit another cigarette. "How long," he asked presently, "do you suppose Shorty lived through that?"

"He lived through all of it."

The guy shivered. "How do you know that?"

"They quit when he quit."

"I see. Okay. Now tell me why."

"I don't know why," Bolan replied. "They could have been punishing him for some indiscretion. Or it could have been an interrogation."

"Shorty wasn't that tough—for that kind of interrogation, I mean. He'd have told them anything they wanted to know from the first slap."

"That wouldn't have mattered," Bolan said quietly.

"It wouldn't have *mattered?*"

Bolan slowly shook his head. "The idea is to break the mind completely through fear, shock, agony, horror—complete carnal degradation. They take a guy completely apart, a piece at a time. They know they're getting to the home twenty when the victim begins confessing long-forgotten childhood sins—masturbation, secret fantasies, stolen cookies, and malicious wishes. They bust the mind, cowboy—wide open and shrieking out everything that ever got lodged in there."

Reynolds took another quick trip to the toilet. He returned a few minutes later and said to Bolan, "Okay, go on."

"Sure you want me to?"

"Yeah. I find that my mad is just getting a head on it. Go on."

Bolan continued, matter-of-factly. "The body breaks down long before the mind does. The voluntary nervous system is usually the first to go. Controls, mostly. Saliva, kidneys, bowels. That adds to the sense of degradation—and only brings on more pain as punishment for the mess. And the guy is already screaming out everything his mind can seize. He's trying to please them, see—trying to get them to stop doing what they're doing. The turkey-maker becomes God himself, and this is the final judgment. But the more the poor guy talks and screams and pleads, the more they put it to him. There's no way out, see, absolutely no relief—except to die. And these guys know what they're doing. They know when to press and when to let up for a moment, when to cut and when to patch, and they're playing the poor guy for every breath of life he has in him. That's a turkey interrogation, cowboy."

Reynolds groaned, "Why do they want to hear all that shit?"

"They figure they have to get it all before they *know* they got anything at all. It's sort of like pouring out a box of cereal to get to a few raisins that are mixed up inside. You can't just rummage through the box for them. You have to pour it all out."

"It's not human," Reynolds muttered.

"Of course it's not human. When did I say I was talking about humans?"

"You really feel that way, don't you?"

"I feel that way," Bolan assured him.

"How many guys like Shorty have you run into?"

"Too many. Shorty was a lucky one. He was in hell for a few hours at the most. Sometimes this stuff goes on for days on end."

"How *could* it?"

"I told you. Some of these guys become real experts, absolute artists at keeping the flesh alive and cringing. I've just been talking about interrogation turkeys. If punishment is their game—well, hell . . ." Bolan's voice became a bit choked. "I knew a cute kid once who lived for fifty days."

"Don't tell me any more," Reynolds said.

"It could happen to you, guy."

The trucker's eyes jerked and flared.

Bolan nodded his head, watching the guy closely. "It's something you have to face up to if you mean to challenge hell."

"Have you faced up to it?"

"Long ago," Bolan told him. "Many, many nightmares ago."

"And still you go on."

"I have to go on."

A tense silence descended. Bolan sipped his coffee and toyed with a cigarette. The trucker stared at his hands, ignoring all else. After a while he said, "Thanks, Big B."

"You're welcome, cowboy."

"It must be tough to talk about."

"It is."

"Thanks. I understand. I still want to go on."

Bolan nodded his head, agreeing with the decision. "You could be between the devil and the deep, anyway. If those guys didn't get satisfaction from Shorty, they just might decide to look for it in Shorty's partner."

The guy's eyes quivered again. He said, "Remember what I told you, back on the ridge when we first met? I said that maybe I owed you more than you realize. I was talking about the contraband. But what if I hadn't gone looking for you? What if I'd gone on to the home twenty and found those goons waiting for me there? Well, hey—I guess I owed you more than I realized."

"It's a curious world," Bolan said softly.

"Yeah. Okay. Where do we go from here?"

"A question, first," Bolan said. His eyes were

hard, probing. "The answer won't affect our friendship. It *could* affect our future—both of us. So say it straight. Were you and Shorty running any kind of knockdown operation on those guys?"

"Not that I know of," Reynolds replied evenly.

"Which means . . ."

"I guess I can't honestly answer for Shorty. Like I told you, things have been a bit out of whack between us since the superskate entered the picture."

"What would be your gut guess?" Bolen persisted.

"I could have answered a few months ago, straight from the gut, no sweat. Now—well, I can only say . . . maybe."

Bolan sighed and finished his coffee. Then he asked, "You feeling okay?"

"Yeah, I'm okay."

"All right." Bolan pushed a miniature tape recorder at the guy. "Sit there and think out loud. Everything you can remember about Shorty after he met the superskate, anything at all that seemed peculiar at the time—or anything that seemed natural at the time but now, in the back-think, seems peculiar. Everything about the girl, absolutely everything that you know or think you know. Anything and everything you can recall about the operations at Bluebird, unusual hauls, offbeat destinations, that sort of thing. Are you game?"

"Sure, I'm game," the trucker replied. "But, hell, it's going to take the rest of the night."

"That's all right," Bolan told him. "Just keep at it. Stay put, right here, until I get back. Don't make any phone calls and don't answer any. Don't show yourself outside the cabin."

"Are you leaving?"

"For a while, yeah. Couple of calls to make before daylight. If I should need to contact you, I'll call three times in quick succession. You'll get two rings on each call. Answer the fourth call. And don't say a thing until you hear my voice."

The guy seemed a bit flustered, but he said, "Okay."

Bolan donned the Beretta shoulder rig, drew on a light jacket, and dropped a few extra clips into a pocket. "I'll move your tractor, in case anyone is searching for it."

"Sure." Reynolds handed him the keys. "Think you can handle it?"

"I'll figure it out," Bolan said, smiling soberly. "And remember, cowboy, you're in total isolation."

The guy gave a weak grin and a shiver. "Never fear," he said.

Bolan went outside and gazed at the stars for a moment while his eyes adjusted to the darkness.

Yeah. The guy would be all right. The routine with the tape recorder was little more than a bit of disguised therapy. By dawn, Reynolds would be ready for the challenge.

By dawn, yeah, the guy would have realized where his guts went, after 'Nam and why he'd been a loser ever since.

By dawn, the fates willing, Mack Bolan would have another soldier on his side.

5: The Promise

The time was nearly five in the morning, and the mansion on Paces Ferry Road was ablaze with lights. A dozen or so cars were parked in a neat line along the circular drive. The house chief, Mellini the Mick—so called because he had once used the alias Mickey Harrigan—paced nervously across the porch with an unlit cigarette dangling from his lips. He came to a sudden halt, frowning at the sound of another vehicle coming up the drive, and stepped behind a column of the porch with a hand resting on the bulge at his coat front.

A taxicab pulled in beneath the portico.

The passenger paid his fare and got out. He was wearing an expensive leisure suit with a safari jacket, soft white shoes, oval glasses with large yellow lenses. He carried a small utility bag emblazoned with an airline's decals.

Eyes hard and body taut, Mellini went quickly down the steps to meet the new arrival.

Before a word could be said, the visitor opened his wallet to show the house boss a miniature playing card, an ace of spades, and announced, "I just got in from the Big Apple. Who's inside?"

Mellini was immediately impressed. A bit of excitement flowed with his voice as he replied, "It's an area conference, sir. They're all here. Have you heard about the Bolan thing?"

The visitor said, "It's why I'm here. That guy is my specialty. You must be Mellini."

The torpedo was surprised and pleased with the make. "Yes, sir, I'm him."

"Heard good of you, Mellini. You call me Frankie."

"Sure, Frankie. Thanks for the—thanks."

"You have any boys on the grounds?"

"Well, no, not yet. We just—"

"Better put a couple on the prowl. Put a couple of cars out, too. You got radios?"

"Sure, we got radios."

"Okay, get a couple of cars out patrolling this neighborhood. They keep in constant touch. And they report any suspicious movements."

"Yes, sir, uh . . ."

"Uh, what?"

"That's going to leave us a little thin on the house detail. We weren't expecting a—I mean, it's been quiet and peaceful around here. We're not up to war strength."

"You will be."

"Well, see, that's what they're talking—oh, okay, yeah, I see what you mean. How many did you bring?"

"Enough. They'll be along soon as they get roomed and all. Put your boys out. It'll be okay."

They were moving up the steps toward the porch.

Mellini said, "Maybe I should wait 'til your boys get here. It's going to be mighty thin here until then."

"You're here, Mickey, and I'm here," the visitor pointed out.

The torpedo laughed softly as he opened the door and ushered the distinguished guest inside. "Well, you're the specialist," he said, yielding to superior authority.

"Step in and let the man know I'm here. I don't want to bust up his conference. Just whisper in his ear. Tell him I brought twenty guns and he should rest easy. I'm taking it over. He can pass that on to his people in there and they can take it into their planning. Tell him I said that. He should go on with his business as though I'm not here."

"Okay, sure," Mellini agreed—almost, it seemed, with a rush of relief. "Uh . . . what should I tell—*who* should I tell him—"

"Just tell him Frankie from the Commission. That's all he needs to know."

"Oh, sure, right, I understand."

The house chief left the guest standing alone in the foyer and made quick tracks toward closed double-doors across the way.

"Mickey!"

The house boss halted and turned back with, "Yeah, Frankie?"

"Where's the kitchen? I'll get some coffee."

"Oh, hell, I'm sorry," Mellini apologized. He raised his voice and called, "*Henry!*"

A handsome old black man, dressed in formal houseservant attire, appeared at an arched doorway at the rear.

"Get Mr. Frank some coffee. Make him feel at home."

Mellini paused at the double doors to watch Henry and the impressive super-hard visitor from New York move off in the direction of the kitchen. Then he crossed his heart, opened the door, and went to tell the good news to the boss of Atlanta.

Mack the Black Ace from New York Bolan accepted the coffee from the old man and said, "Thanks, Henry. Has Miss Rossiter gone to bed?"

"Oh, yes, suh—I would say so, suh."

He was a black gentleman of the old Southern school—a truly class guy, in his way.

The Bolan face was reflecting regret and indecision as he said, "Guess I'll have to wake her up. Would you?—no, I'd better do it myself. Where's her room?"

"You won't have no trouble knowing it, suh. They got a gentleman standing at the do'. They wouldn't let me in there, nohow."

A class guy, yeah. And a hell of a lot smarter than the house boss.

The two men stared at each other through a moment of revealing silence, then Bolan asked, "How long have you served this household, Henry?"

"Just since—not long, suh."

"Any more servants here?"

"Two colored ladies, suh."

"You go get those ladies, Henry, and you take them away from here. Understand me? Take them away, quick and far."

The old man's eyes rustled. "I knew there was trouble, Mistuh Frank."

"Very soon it will be the end of troubles, Henry. You don't want to be here when that time comes."

"No, suh, we sho' don't."

"Do it now. Right now."

Bolan left the old gentleman in the kitchen. He carried his coffee with him as he returned to the entry hall and went up the stairs to the second floor.

A sleepy-eyed punk was slouched on a wooden chair at a closed door about halfway along the upstairs corridor. He snapped upright and reached for the coffee as Bolan approached.

"Hey, thanks," he said thickly. "I need that."

"So do I," Bolan said coldly. He showed the guy his calling card instead, and told him, "Mick wants you downstairs, kid—on the double."

The youngster's eyes did a cartoon-character roll at sight of the black ace. He scrambled to his feet, upsetting the chair and apologizing under his breath as he backed away from there—pausing at the head of the stairs for a clumsy wave before hurrying below.

Bolan was strictly playing by ear and had been since the moment he stepped onto this enemy turf. Every word and action, to this point, had been dictated by sheer instinct plus the vibrations of the place. There was no coherent plan of action, other than to get into that house and run with the vibrations. He was doing precisely that.

A small bed lamp was providing muted illumination to a luxuriously feminine apartment. The bed itself was rumpled and empty. Miss Superskate, he presumed, was reclining comfortably on a large chair near the window. She was softly svelte, stunningly blonde, and glowing in the semi-darkness . . . utterly naked.

The great eyes were wide open, alert, and seemingly quite unperturbed by the invasion of her privacy.

Bolan placed the coffee on a table and went to the window.

"You're a new one," declared the soft voice behind him. A nice voice, yeah, interested and alive—not frightened, not angry, but not exactly relaxed either.

"I'm the last one," he told her, "if that's the way you want it. I can take you out of here."

She had made no move toward modesty.

"Where would you take me?"

He flexed his eyes and said, "Just out. The rest would be up to you."

She sighed. "At long last my prince has come. Is that the new routine? Don't you people ever get tired of this?"

He turned to look her over, doing so quite honestly and thoroughly. And, yeah, there should have been a lot of truck accidents in this region.

She did not shrink from nor respond to that inspection.

He bent over to place a gentle hand on that soft belly, and still there was no response.

When the hand came away, a medal remained to cover the navel impression.

He told her, quietly, "I'm tired of it already. There's no time for a hard sell. You either trust me or you don't, leave with me or you don't."

Her hand moved to the bull's-eye cross and she held it to the light. "What is this?"

"It's a marksman's medal."

Something crossed that fixed gaze, some emotion, a flicker of something. She said, quietly, "How can I believe this?"

He shrugged and told her, "I can't help you with that."

"How will you get me out?"

"We'll walk—quiet and easy—out the door and into the night."

"Just like that."

He displayed a half-smile. "Just like that."

"What about my sister?"

"What about her?"

She sighed again. "Forget it. She won't leave him."

"Your sister is Mrs. Sciaparelli?"

"You didn't know that?"

Bolan experienced one of those shivery moments when the self seems to partition into two, with one part standing aside and viewing the self from a completely detached point of view. The experience itself was weird enough; that which was being viewed was even weirder. There he stood, at the chair of a naked golden goddess whom he had just chanced upon while strolling through a strange house, the life or death decision at each heartbeat, chatting inanely, neither behaving as though they knew the lady was naked.

The moment flared and died, and Bolan heard himself saying: "No, but it explains a few things. I have some unpleasant news for you. They got to Shorty. He's dead."

Those great eyes recoiled and took a dive, the chin falling with them onto that magnificent chest.

Bolan said, "I'm sorry. I felt that you should know."

When the eyes came up again, they were moist and pained. "It's okay," she whispered. "I was half resigned to it."

Irrationally, perhaps, the statement irritated him. He said, "Good for you. Now Shorty can rest easy."

"I know how it sounded," she said with a quick sigh. "I didn't mean it that way. I just—"

"My numbers are gone," he said coldly. "I have to go, with or without you."

She immediately slid from the chair, moved cat-like to a closet, selected a simple dress, and dropped it over her shoulders. It was all she put on. "Let's go, then," she said.

Bolan tossed her a pair of sandals. "You might be glad you wore these," he told her.

She gave him a brief, thoughtful gaze and then put the sandals on. He took her hand, and they went into the corridor.

"I need to tell Suzy," she whispered.

Bolan shook his head at that. "Call her later," he suggested, and led her on along the hall and down the stairs.

They were halfway home when Sciaparelli stepped into the foyer. He was a guy of about forty—lean and hard, very mean in the eyes. That cold gaze bounced from the girl to the man as he asked, "What is this?"

"You know what it is," Bolan replied coldly, still playing to the vibes. "Don't make this any harder than it has to be."

The guy stood his ground. "What do you want with her, Frankie?"

"You know what we want, Ship. Don't worry about it. She will get all the respect you deserve. We just want a few gentle words."

"You can have the words, Frankie. But you take them right here. She stays."

"This doesn't look good, Ship," the black ace said quietly.

The girl was beginning to appear confused, shaken. She asked her brother-in-law, "Who is this man, Charles?"

"He's from the gestapo," Sciaparelli muttered. The guy was caving in. "Cooperate with him. You'd better. He's not married to your sister." The guy spun away and walked quickly toward the conference room.

Bolan moved the capo's sister-in-law on toward the front door. "Good girl," he said softly, lips at her ear. "You played that perfectly."

But she hadn't been "playing it." The young lady was terrified now. She planted her feet and tried to twist free of Bolan's grasp, sobbing with the effort and making a hell of a fuss.

Mellini ran into the foyer and rebuked the lady. "Stop that, Jenny! Behave yourself!" He gave Bolan a sympathetic wink and opened the door for him.

Bolan winked back as he lifted the lady off her feet and carried her outside. The struggling had ceased, but he could feel her pounding heart.

"You'll need some wheels," the house boss said, following them through the doorway to the porch. "You want to use her car? It's a real boat."

Bolan replied, "Okay. Bring it around, will you?"

The guy happily trotted away, returning a moment later, with a screech of tires, revving the powerful engine. He held the door for them as Bolan placed his load inside then closed it and stood guard while the visiting V.I.P. went to the other side.

Their eyes met across the convertible roof. The house boss reminded the black ace: "It's getting thinner here, Frankie."

"It'll be okay," the visitor reassured him. "My boys will be along soon."

"What do I tell them?—when they ask about you, I mean."

"Tell them not to ask," Bolan said. He climbed in, meshed the gears, and put that joint behind him.

The girl was subdued, silent, sullen.

As they were crossing Peachtree Road, Bolan asked the lady, "What did you expect me to do, Jennifer? Show the guy a marksman's medal and shoot our way out? I told you we were walking."

She said, tiredly, "It's very confusing."

"If you think you're confused," he replied, "how do you think those people back there are going to feel when they begin to wake up?"

She was evidently thinking about it, and the thought was giving her the quiet giggles.

He put a gentle hand to her and said, "That's better."

"I'm sorry. I can't stop."

"It's okay."

She seized his arm with both hands and clung to it.

It was okay, sure. Mild hysteria was a far better consequence than that suffered by the late Shorty Wilkins. And Bolan was quite positive that this beautiful young woman had been a prime candidate for the same fate.

"It's okay," he told her again.

It was a promise, not a mere comforting remark.

She snuggled to him, flowing across the console to bury her face in his shoulder.

And that, it seemed to the warrior, was a promise of quite another sort.

It was, yeah, promising to be a hell of an interesting war.

6: Contact

Bolan brought the lady some coffee in a paper cup then watched her through the glass of the telephone booth as he made his call to an unlisted number in Washington.

A sleepy voice responded to the fifth ring.

Bolan told it, "This is Striker and it's hot."

"Hold it," was the quick response, that voice alert now and cautious. "Give me a number and let me call you back."

"No way," Bolan replied. "If your own bedroom isn't clean, what is?"

"We never know, these days," was the tired response. "It's okay, Striker—hold it just a minute. I can switch it over from here. Hold on."

Bolan held on while the Number Two Cop in the country played his games with communications security. The caution was understandable. The relationship between Mack Bolan and Harold Brognola was a strictly unofficial one—even a perilous one, for the Justice Department high-ranker.

"Okay," Brognola said, following a series of squeals and clicks on the line. "I'm on the clean line. How are things in Georgia?"

"You've heard then."

"Oh, sure. Every shoe you drop, friend, is a shot heard round the world. To what do I owe this direct contact with the esteemed King of Swat?"

Bolan chuckled soberly as he told his friend, "I don't like these contacts any more than you do, Hal. But I need a favor and I need it quick."

"Name it," Brognola said. "Anything but my wife, my job, or my life."

"I need a direct line to someone in this area. Do you have a local who would play the game and keep it quiet?"

A brief silence preceded the JD man's reply. "I think—maybe, yeah. But you'll have to set it up yourself. If the guy tells you he'll play, then you can believe him."

"FBI field-office type?"

"No, hell no. There's too many layers between me and those guys. Do you have pencil and paper?"

"Yeah, go ahead."

Brognola passed him a name and a telephone number, adding, "He's young, he's bright, and he's hot to trot. Just might be your man. But you can't mention my name, Striker. So do it carefully."

"Understood," Bolan assured him. "Thanks."

"Don't mention it. I'll be watching that area with great interest. Let me know if this contact doesn't pan out for you."

"I'll do that."

"This seems to be my night for illicit calls. Sticker called a couple of hours ago. Says he's been trying to reach you."

"I've been off the floater for a while," Bolan explained. "What's he got?"

"Sticker" was one Leo Turrin, another Bolan buddy with sensitive connections. Turrin was underboss of a powerful Eastern family. He was also an undercover cop working directly under Brognola.

"Just the usual warnings," the JD man growled. "The old men are fielding another elite force to defend Atlanta."

"Did he pass you the info?"

"Yeah. The headman is a black ace who is currently known as Domino. He's bringing a crew of headhunters from the special corps, scheduled to land down there about six o'clock. That's less than an hour from now. You're on Eastern time, huh?"

"Yeah."

"Okay, they're looking at you, friend. Sticker says to expect about two dozen guns—all top hands."

"How are they traveling? Private plane?"

"Company jet, yeah. You want the registry number?"

"Why not?" Bolan took the number and said, "Thanks, Hal. I'll see if I can shake a plum loose for you down here."

"Everything you shake is a plum for me, friend. Just cover your butt."

"It's not my butt they want, Hal. I'm not that pretty."

"Well, cover the other end, too. And get in

touch with the Sticker as soon as you can. He worries, you know."

"Not like us, eh."

"Right. Not like us."

It was the typical end of a conversation between the two. Bolan grinned into the disconnect and hung up, rejoining the lady in the superskate.

It was a Corvette, after all—though not a stock model—with more direct power than any car ought to have. It was the only car in Bolan's experience that seemed to have a head and heart of its own. It did not like to idle or dawdle. It wanted to roar, and actually seemed to resist any effort to restrain it.

He smiled at the lady, fired the engine, and roared away from there. When they had climbed into a cruising gear and the G-forces had fallen away, he asked her, "What's the running time from here to the airport?"

"Are you sending me away?"

He shook his head. "I'd like to be there for a six o'clock arrival."

She consulted the dashboard clock, then suggested, "Jump over onto 285. Uh, turn right at the next light."

The surface streets at this hour of the morning seemed entirely deserted. They made it to the interstate bypass route in three minutes flat, with a minimum of conversation along the way.

"How did you do it?" she asked him.

"Do what?"

"You just walked into that house and took it over. You had them bowing and scraping, jumping to your slightest wish. Even Charles called you by another name. How did you do that?"

He explained it to her as succinctly as possible. "It's hocus-pocus, sleight of hand. You give them what they expect to see and hear. And you're playing to their own secret rituals. It's the price they pay for their own dumb intrigue."

"But they were looking right at you and didn't even recognize you."

"What's to recognize? A face is just a face—until you connect a personality to it. That's where the sleight of hand comes in."

"*I'd* never forget that face," she quietly observed.

He chuckled and told her, "*I'll* never forget that body. I admire your sleight of hand, too, lady breaker."

She giggled, and confided to him, "Well, it kept them at a distance. After all, I do have a certain status around that house."

It explained, to Bolan's satisfaction at the moment, the household nudity—but all the disturbing questions had not been put to rest.

And as they headed up the ramp to join the light traffic of the freeway, the lady turned on her CB radio and picked up the mike.

"Okay?" she queried him. "I'll use a false handle. And we can find out where the Smokies are. We don't want a traffic cop at a time like this."

Bolan grinned and said, "Why not?"

Her voice sounded quite different, and even the facial expression underwent a total transformation as she depressed the mike button and went to work on the knights of the road. "Break, nineteen," she cooed. "How 'bout a northbound eighteen-wheeler on this 285."

A guy came right back, in a singsong style peculiar to truckers with long, boring hours behind the wheel.

"Hello there, sweet thing. You've got the Howling Owl, trucking north from Orlando with the pedal to the metal. Bring it on back and brighten my life for a short-short."

The girl grinned at Bolan as she responded to that in a shivery little voice. "Just loving you for that comeback, Howling Owl. You've got the Evening Star, running light and sassy on the southbound and looking to spread my light in every heart. Take a look over your shoulder there, lover boy, and tell me what you see."

"Mercy me!" the guy drooled back. "I said brighten my life, sweet thing, not blind me off the superslab. What are you driving, Evening Star?"

"Business first," she insisted. "What've you got over your shoulder, lover?"

"Mercy goodness, I think I forget, for sure. Aw, naw, I wouldn't fool you, darling. I haven't seen a Smoky all night. You've got it clean all the way to the Florida line—unless you'd like to coffee break with me. You want to sugar my coffee before you face that lonesome road again?"

The sexy lady giggled into the mike as she told the Howling Owl, "I'll catch you on the flip-flop sometime, lover. I could kiss you for that info, so consider it done. The Evening Star is clear and on the side, sallying south."

"Thank you for the short-short, darling, and here's all those good numbers back at you. We gone. Bye-bye."

She put the mike down and told Bolan, "Punch it. You're clean."

He said, "So I gathered." But he was giving the

'Vette all the "punch" he wanted her to have. "We have plenty of time."

"Chicken," she said playfully, "you didn't like my radio personality either, did you?"

He shrugged and told her, "It must sound great on the other end."

"It's just a fun game," she said, turning away from him to stare soberly at the windshield.

"Hey—it's your radio and your car," he told her soothingly. "You don't need my approval."

"That's right, I don't. Nor anyone else's. But what's wrong with it? Tell me. It's a game, and everyone knows it's a game. Why, I could never talk to a man like that, face to face. I'd bust out laughing if I tried. But this way, see—it's anonymous. The handle is just another form of alias. And that's what makes it fun. Do you use the CB much?"

"Not much," Bolan replied.

"Then that's why you don't understand."

"I understand," he protested feebly.

"No, you don't." She seemed to feel the need to vindicate her point—or perhaps herself. "I have a theory. I believe it reveals the basic nature of man."

"What does?" he idly inquired.

"The CB phenomenon. It is, you know. A phenomenon. I mean, in CB-land, it's nothing but good buddies everywhere. Everybody is kind and friendly, outgoing, helpful, and warm. I used to wonder about it. I used to think that only the best people had CB radios, because they were all like that. Then one day I had the shock of my life. I discovered that one of my good road buddies was the same horrible old man who lives down the street from me. I mean, he is a *pill*—grumpy, crabby, chases little kids off his lawn—just a horrible old beast. But, oh what a lover he is on the CB. Not just to me. It doesn't have anything to do with me. He's like that to everybody when he's in his car and talking to them on the radio. You know what his handle is? It's Pussy Cat. And that's just what he is, really, a pussy cat. He can reveal himself, see, on the radio—his true self—because nobody knows that he doubles as the Beast of Paces Ferry Road."

"That's your theory, eh?"

"In a nutshell, yes. Everyone would prefer to be kind and cheerful and friendly. That's the basic instinct. We assume nasty roles in life for various reasons that I'm sure the psychologists could explain. But when we can hide behind a handle, see, and we're nothing but a voice on a radio—nobody really knows who we are, see—then we have no use for the nasty role and we can just be our natural friendly selves. It's sort of like what you were saying about sleight of hand, except reversed."

Bolan said, "That's interesting. I'll think about it."

"Sex is the same way."

It caught him a bit off guard. He said, "What?" for lack of anything else to say.

"Sex is best when it's anonymous."

He chuckled. "Well, I couldn't say. I've never tried that. Have you?"

A bit defiantly, she replied, "Yes, I have."

That was apparently all she had to say about it for the moment, and Bolan did not care to probe the subject—at the moment.

They observed a silence until the airport lights came into veiw.

"There you are," she said. "Take the next exit."

He said, "Thanks."

"Don't mention it. Do you have a CB handle?"

He replied, "I guess not."

"I could give you one. I'll bet it should be Superstud."

Bolan said, "Thanks."

"Don't mention it. Why are we going to the airport?"

"I need to eyeball a head party."

"What?"

He explained, "Some people are coming down here to collect my head. I want to see who they are."

She said, "Maybe not."

"What?"

"My theory. Maybe it doesn't apply to everyone equally."

"Which theory, now, are we retracting?"

"Both of them. I'll wait and see. I'll check you later."

Bolan grinned and pulled onto the airport exit.

The conversation with the lady had developed hardly any intelligence. But there would be time enough for that, later. The important thing, for the moment, was that a relationship of some confidence—however frivolous—had been established between himself and the sister-in-law of the boss of Atlanta.

And, yeah, it was getting to be a hell of an interesting war.

7: Eyeballed

It was among the busiest airports in the country, sure, but there was very little bustle in any airport at this hour of the day. Bolan drifted along with the thin movement of people until he spotted a security cop. He grabbed the guy and maneuvered him into a corner where he flashed an I.D. wallet as he announced, "I'm on short time and I need some quick info. Where would a private jet, a big jet, be likely to unload passengers?"

The cop gave him a dumb look. "You'd have to check with the airlines," he replied.

"I said private jet, guy. Where do they off-load the non-commercial flights?"

"Hell, I don't—why don't you check with the office?"

"Who's in charge of the shift?" Bolan snapped impatiently.

"Captain Newly—Jim Newly—you take the—it's next floor down; go on around the corner and—"

"I'll find it," Bolan growled. He studied the guy's badge in a rather deliberating fashion then dropped his voice to a low pitch to say: "Between us Indians, what do you think about Newly? Could I count on his cooperation for a Federal bust? I'm going to need help, and there's no time to get it elsewhere."

The cop was hung somewhere between a smile and a frown. "Blow on his gun," he replied quietly. "He'll lead you anywhere."

"Eager beaver, huh?"

"That's putting it mildly."

Bolan squeezed the guy's shoulder and went on. Time was running away, and there was nothing to do now but follow the play. He found the security office at ten minutes before the hour. A couple of uniformed officers were checking notices on a bulletin board, and a young lady in a coffee-stained blouse was working at an open file cabinet. The door to an inner office stood open, revealing a guy in a rumpled wash-and-wear suit having coffee and doughnuts over the morning newspaper.

Bolan sized the guy as he went on past the uniforms and walked into the office. He was somewhere on the sunny side of forty, medium height and build—a bit soft around the edges maybe but a face like a domesticated wolf.

Yeah, maybe.

"You Newly?" he asked, as the guy took note of his presence.

"That's me. What'll you have?"

Bolan opened the I.D. wallet and held it at shoulder level. "Mackey, Treasury," he identified himself, closing the wallet and returning it to his pocket in one deft motion. "Don't get up—one quick request." He handed the guy a slip of paper. "It's a private jet, arriving from New York. Should be in the airport control zone right now. I'd like to know where she'll be off-loading her passengers."

"That should be easy," the guy said. He reached for his phone and called the control tower, chatted for a moment, then hung up and casually passed the information on to his visitor. "What else will you have, uh, uh . . ."

"Mackey."

"Right."

Bolan seemed to be wavering over some decision. He said, "Well, it's just a routine surveillance. If you have a couple of men to spare, though, for a few minutes—uh, I'm not expecting any trouble but—uh, well, maybe just in case."

The cop grinned and got to his feet. "No problem at all," he assured the visitor. "I'll go along, too. What'd you say your name is again?" ·

Bolan told him again.

"Right. Want a doughnut, Mackey?"

Boland politely declined the hospitality.

"Guess we better get going then," the cop said. He took his coffee with him and collected the two uniformed officers as he moved through the outer office.

Once started, the guy was a fast mover. Bolan fell into step beside him and said, "I appreciate this, Newly."

"Forget it. It's my territory. I wouldn't want anything going down without my look-see, anyway. Right?"

"Right," Bolan soberly agreed with the eager beaver.

"What *is* going down, Mackey? No bullshit, now. What is it?"

Bolan was being very restrained about the whole thing. "We just want a make on those passengers," he assured the guy.

"Yeah, bullshit," the guy replied to that. "I asked you what is going down. What division of Treasury are you with? And don't say Secret Service because I can spot those guys from the end of a long runway."

Bolan grinned and confided in the guy: "There's, uh, this very hot war, you know, in Ireland."

Yeah. With this guy, it wasn't what you said but what you didn't say. He had a quick mind, and it moved instantly to its own conclusion.

"Guns, huh. You saying they're trying to move them through this airport?"

Bolan kept the restraint intact. "I didn't say that, Newly. But there's a connection here, yeah— we're sure of that."

"You want me to provide some muscle—here and now? Why not? We should have a look inside that plane."

Already it was "we."

"Nothing that obvious, no, not at this stage of the thing, Newly. Of course, while I'm eyeballing them, if *you* should happen to note a local violation of some sort . . ."

The guy had already taken the hook and now he was about to swallow it.

"Just who are these people, Mackey? No bullshit, now. It's my airport, and I have a right to know what's moving through it. What's moving through my airport, Mackey?"

They had arrived at the designated area. This part of the terminal was utterly deserted. A large window overlooked an aircraft ramp and service area; a metal door beside the window provided access. They were at ground level.

"Will they be coming through that door?" Bolan inquired.

"No. They'll exit to this side and walk around the tail of the plane to that other building. You didn't answer me, Mackey. Who are they?"

"It's a mob operation, Newly."

The guy was very impressed with that bit of news. He looked at his two uniformed officers with a quick grin and declared, "That's fair game, isn't it?"

"It works both ways," Bolan suggested. "Don't try these guys, Newly."

"How many people are we talking about?"

"A bunch," Bolan assured him. "We think they're attending a regional meet."

The guys eyes went to full red alert. The voice was low and controlled, though, as he said, "It figures. Have you heard about the wingding just north of here last night?"

Bolan quietly replied, "Oh, yeah. We heard."

The airport cop took a transistor radio from a belt clip and began calling for reinforcements.

Bolan said, half angrily, "What the hell are you doing?"

"Back off, T-Man," Newly growled back. "It's my airport and my responsibility to control it. You do your job and I'll do mine. And maybe I'll be doing yours for you. You came out to get an eyeball. Okay. Maybe I'll give you a good long one. How would you like to have fingerprints and the whole smear?"

"You'll have egg on your face, Newly!"

"So I love eggs; I'm crazy about them!" the cop snarled. "Stay out of my way, Mackey, and out of my hair!"

The company plane was now in view, moving smoothly along the taxiway toward the unloading area.

Uniformed cops were running in from every direction, and a couple of cars with flashing lights were on an intersecting course with the plane.

Very quietly, Bolan told the hip-shooter, "This is all on your head, Newly. Unless you call off that horde of plastic cops, I have no option but to withdraw completely. I mean it."

"I'll show you plastic cops," Newly growled. He began issuing crisp instructions through the radio—placing his men, setting it up.

The guy may have been an eager sucker for a Bolan con job, but there was no taking it away from him—he knew his business. He went outside, still working at the radio, as the plane rolled to a halt.

Bolan grinned, lit a cigarette, and took his ringside observation station at the big window.

There would be no shoot-out here, Bolan was positive of that. The enemy knew their business, also—and it did not involve senseless gun battles with airport security cops. Not these boys, anyway. They would suffer the indignities and bulldoze their way clear with legal finesse, not with fireworks.

The hassle, though, would take away their cutting edge for a while, imbalance their fine footwork, and perhaps provide Bolan with a crack to work on.

He stood at his post and watched the Newly Patrol do their job as the debarkation of a head party began.

The first guy down was packing a piece under his coat. Bolan mentally photographed that face and carefully watched the body language as the torpedo was roughly seized and frisked. Aloof from it all, yeah, above it—cool and self-possessed, a true pro from the head shed—quietly submitting with frozen face and uncommitted eyes.

At twenty minutes past six, twenty-two carbon copies of the guy had been "processed" on the ground, and a couple of cops had entered the aircraft in search of more.

Newly stepped inside and approached Bolan with a forgiving grin. "What, you still here, T-Man? I thought you had withdrawn."

"You run a slick bust, Newly," Bolan complimented him. "Now what?"

"Now nothing," the cop said airily. "They're all carrying court credentials and gun permits. Can you beat it? A Federal judge gave those torpedoes a license to kill. I'm going to search the cargo hold, just the same, and I'm going to document every damn thing I see. Come by the office tomorrow. I'll have copies made up for you."

"Do that," Bolan said. His eyes had not left the window.

"What are you waiting for?"

"Someone's missing," Bolan told him. "The top dog hasn't come out yet."

It was at that moment that Bolan spotted his man, just then emerging from the plane, sandwiched between two uniformed cops.

A total stranger, yeah, but a black ace as surely as though an identifying label had been sewn to his coat lapel. The make was there in the stance, the way he moved, the cut of the clothes, the way the eyes focused nowhere but obviously saw everything.

Gazes clashed, nevertheless, at the window for a brief instant, and Bolan knew that a double make, of sorts, had been made in that moment.

"There's your guy, Newly," he said icily. "Run him through your grinder and don't miss a thing. Find out who he really is, and you'll never forget this day."

The cop's gaze was traveling curiously back and forth between the man outside and the one inside, beside him. There was puzzlement there, in that gaze, growing gradually and trying to crystallize into some deeper understanding.

Bolan respected the guy too much to play him longer. He shook hands, said, "Good work, guy," and went quickly away from there.

The war for Atlanta was heating up.

Bolan needed to set his army and establish his lines before the enemy could outmaneuver him.

He needed to do some scouting and develop some hard intelligence before the same-side soldiers closed off all his avenues.

And he needed to fulfill the expectations of a couple of non-combatants who, unless he moved very carefully, could nevertheless become grim casualties of the conflict.

He returned to the hot Corvette and told the sexy lady, "Okay, Miss Superskate, grab your radio. *Now* it's time to punch it."

Oh, yeah. It had become a very interesting war.

8: Of Friends and Foes

The new chief of the Federal strike force in Georgia may have been a bit young for the position, but none of his older and more experienced people had found cause to challenge his weight for the job. Sharp of mind and quick of step, David Ecclefield was a public servant who would neither allow moss to collect beneath his body nor cobwebs to gather inside his skull. And he was tough, yes—a very tough cop who would not be easily swerved aside by technicalities peculiar to his profession.

All the same, it had been a frustrating assignment for "Young David" since his arrival in the Peachtree State. During a recent conference with his superiors in Washington, he had thumped the table with exasperation while "educating the Wonderland Wizards" into the problems of crime-fighting in the new South.

"Forget all that stuff!" he'd told them angrily. "This isn't the 'way-down-South land of cotton' we're talking about here! Scarlett O'Hara and Rhett Butler are a hundred years in the past. The city of Atlanta today has a *black mayor*. The metropolitan population is ranked with the top twenty of the country. It's the industrial capital of the Southeast, a major distribution hub, and cultural center of the whole damned South.

"It's not the home of Uncle Remus and ol' boll weevil—not anymore. It's now the home of Hank Aaron and the Atlanta Braves—not to mention the NFL Falcons, the NBA Hawks, and the NHL Flames. It's big city, gentlemen—a swinging town and entirely sophisticated. The area has more than a thousand manufacturing plants. And diversification? Try airplanes and fertilizers, automobiles and processed foods, steel and paper, chemicals and furniture. The city is served by three major interstate highways. It boasts one of the five busiest airports in the nation. There are three daily newspapers and thirty-eight radio and TV stations. It's a financial center, home of a Federal Reserve district bank. The national Disease Control Center is headquartered there. It is one hell of a complicated, complex, booming area. That's why the mob is there. Do you imagine that they came for ham hocks and grits?

"The Atlanta metro area alone is made up of fifteen different counties and God knows how many small towns. Can you appreciate how many individual police agencies are tied into a hodgepodge like that? I don't have enough men to watch the *cops*! What the hell am I supposed to do with a handful of Federal agents and a couple of legal eagles? Why ask *me* why the crime patterns are enlarging? Take a look at your own statistics. On the Uniform Crime Index, Atlanta sits squarely between New York City and Washington. How many Federal cops do you have here in Washington? How many in New York?"

Quite a speech, sure—daring if not exactly brilliant. It had brought him nothing but frowns, excuses, and vague promises. There would be no help from Washington. Those people up there had their own problems—very unique problems, as it were. The bureau had never been under heavier fire, from more diverse quarters. The entire Department of Justice was sinking into low profile. All the heads were simply trying to maintain the status quo now. The call everywhere was for less Federal government, not for more. So how could a lowly strike-force honcho from the Southland expect to get much more than unofficial sympathy, excuses, and vague promises.

Very early on the third morning after his return from that futile trip to Wonderland, Ecclefield was at his desk at strike headquarters, poring over the police and fire reports of that incident up near Kennesaw. He was a speed-reader, and his retention was very nearly one hundred percent. Nevertheless, he'd already gone over the packet several times when the telephone interrupted his concentration.

His caller displayed a manner that invited respect. The voice was cool without being hostile, aloof without seeming arrogant. It was a voice to respect—one, at least, to listen to.

"Ecclefield here."

"Is your telephone clean, Ecclefield?"

"I hope so. Who is this?"

"It's best that you don't ask. It will come to you as we talk."

"Great. What do we talk about?"

"Organized crime is your business, right?"

"Right. What's yours?"

"The same. From a slightly different viewpoint, you could say. Does the name Charles Sciaparelli have any special meaning for you?"

"You said it, chum. Organized crime *is* my business."

"Here's an item for your block chart. Ship is the invisible man behind the Bluebird operation. It was his hard point. Munitions, booze, junk, that sort of stuff. Are you with me?"

"I'm with you. Can I rely on that information?"

"You can. You won't find the corporate link, but it's there. The proceeds are funneled in through his trust operations and recycled into the software. Look for a financial *wunkerkind* by the name of Walters. He's the pivot man. You'll find the dirty transactions buried in his books, if you can find a way to shake them loose."

"Hold it, I'm trying to jot this—that name is Walters?—with an S?"

"Right. Office in the Five Points area."

"Check. Let's return to Bluebird for a minute. What else can you tell me about that operation?"

"It was a glorious fire."

Ecclefield chuckled. "Uh-huh. Okay. You're the guy, huh?"

"I'm the guy. Do you feel tainted?"

"Not at all. Honored, maybe. Why me?"

"I have to pick them up and put them down very carefully, guy. It's a problem peculiar to my business—a fatal problem, if I guess wrong. I've been told that you wouldn't necessarily be fatal to me."

"Uh-huh. I see. No, I don't see. What is it you're asking?"

"A friendly truce, between your side of the street and mine for a mutual exchange of valuable intelligence."

"That sounds uh . . . that sounds . . ."

"It sounds doubtful, where I'm sitting."

"No, I was just . . . weighing the possible costs."

"No costs, except to your conscience, maybe, if you don't know where it's at. I need a commitment, Ecclefield. Yes or no."

"Yes. Can we get together?"

"Be at Grant Park one hour from now. You'll need a car with a radio, police VHF. Give me a channel, and I'll find it."

They established a communications contact channel, and the guy hung up.

Ecclefield slowly put his phone down then went to the door and called his assistant. He cancelled all standing strike-force assignments and placed the entire crew on headquarters standby. Then he placed calls to two separate offices in the Federal Courthouse, in quick succession; the first to the clerk for a Federal district judge, the second to the local Federal attorney. Both produced highly satisfying results.

Next, he called Washington and bullied his way through to the top man in his chain of command.

"I have a peculiar situation here, Mr. Brognola," he told his chief. "Without going into specifics, I was wondering if I could ask for your counsel."

"You have no friends in Washington, David," his chief advised him.

"Yes, sir. That points up the peculiar situation I find here in Atlanta. It seems that I have found a friend."

"Good for you," Brognola said. "Don't take it lightly."

"Thank you, sir. I am happy to have your understanding."

"That's all you have, David."

"Yes, sir."

Young David hung up the phone, swiveled his chair about, and gazed upon the lovely morning arising over Atlanta. He crossed his feet on the windowsill, lit a cigarette, and said good morning to a whole new ball game.

Twenty minutes removed from downtown Atlanta, in a rather unusual setting, another police conference of sorts was just then getting under way. Participants were from various municipal and county jurisdictions. Their number was precisely one dozen. Some were in uniform, more wore ordinary street clothes. Rank seemed to have little to say about protocol; each seemed to have an equal voice as well as an equal stake in the proceedings. The meeting site was an open field where organized sports for youngsters were conducted according to their season.

The twelve congregated around their vehicles, smoked and passed a bottle in comradely fashion, and discussed in worried tones the problem of the day.

"That's crazy. What can *we* do about the guy? If

all the cops in New York, all the cops in Chicago, all the cops in Los Angeles, all the cops in—"

"Your record's stuck, Billy Bob."

"You get my meaning."

"Meanings won't help much. We need to stop this guy before he wrecks everything."

"Maybe he's already stopped. He made the hit . . . when?—eight, nine hours ago? Maybe he's long gone by now."

"Randy might have something, there. I've got a file drawer full of the guy. He don't spend much time screwing around in one place. Hits and gits. That's why he's so damned hard to catch. When you realize he's there, he's already gone."

"They don't figure to get off that easy. They say if he knew about Bluebird, then he knows about the others. They're worried."

"They should be. Bluebird was the hard point. I bet they lost a lot of money up there last night."

"Millions, you know it. I bet it wasn't even insured."

"Course it wasn't insured. How do you write policy on illegal goods?"

"I figure those guys write anything they want to write. Hell, I bet they own some of those insurance companies."

"Maybe you're right. They own everything else."

"Let's stick to the problem, boys. Is anyone here bleeding for those people? Who gives a shit what *they* lose—except as it's going to hit us? It's *our* territory the guy is messing with."

"The chief is right. We've got to commit to something here."

"I don't know what I'd do without my territory. I just bought that new lemon—that *fuckin'* thing, what a dog. Without my territory, I couldn't even keep up with the garage bills. Forget the damn finance company."

"See, that's our whole problem. That's the nutshell. We've come to depend on all this. What's going to happen if it all falls apart—for even a little while? Henry's banker got it last night, at Kennesaw. Where is Henry's envelope coming from this week? From the grave?"

"I'll scratch something up; don't worry about me."

"That ain't right, Henry. You know that ain't right. I make a motion we set up a fund to cover this. We're all together—right? What hits one hits all. We'll share the bad with the good. Right?"

"We'll talk about that later, Billy Bob. Let's concentrate on one problem at a time. Our problem, right now, is Mack Bolan. We've got to chop the guy."

"I don't like you putting it that way, chief."

"Naw, the chief is right. Might as well say it right out."

"That's right; Henry's right. Nobody is talking about a murder here. We're talking about doing our duty as lawmen."

"Right, but just doing it a little harder."

"We already have everything covered. The damn bulletins say it right out: 'Shoot on sight. Shoot to kill.' Like he said, just try a little harder."

"That's what it comes down to."

"Right."

"This guy, uh, he—they say he don't shoot at badges."

"I hope you don't believe that shit, Billy Bob! I

hope you don't hit those streets at night with a flashlight on your badge, hoping it won't get shot at!"

"Knock it off! I don't need that shit! You know what I was saying."

"We all know what Billy Bob was saying. He's saying he'll feel bad cutting down on the guy. Hell, that's okay, that's human—we're all humans here. But we all know, too, that we've got to stop the guy. Right, Billy Bob?"

"That's what I was saying."

"Okay. We're not making decisions. There is no decision. This is a tactical meeting. We've got to mark the spots and make sure they stay covered. That's our advantage, isn't it? We know the spots. Okay. Night and day, we work it the same as a regular watch rotation. Standard procedures, see. But we *work* it."

"It has to be cool. We don't want to give away the territories. Busted is busted, whether Bolan does it or we do it."

"The chief is right. We have to do it cool."

"Okay. Let's get to work on the assignments."

"Here you go. Use this clipboard. I already got the squads marked up."

"Yeah. Okay. Let's see, now. If we . . ."

And so it went, into the morning of the first day.

If these men had their way, there would be no second day for Mack Bolan along the Dixie Corridor.

9: Fraternity

The official police reaction to the Bolan presence in Georgia took form as a unified tactical reaction force, combining elements of the various metropolitan police agencies as well as representatives from the Georgia Bureau of Investigation.

It was largely a "paper force," with actual staffing limited to a coordinating function—the Reaction Control Center (RCC), headquartered within the Atlanta Police Department.

In theory, it was an impressive force with awesome resources and seemingly limitless applications. There were those critics, however, who doubted that the theory would ever become reality since success depended entirely on mutal cooperation and support from the agencies involved. And it was a diverse lot. There had not been notable success of similar ventures in the past.

For good or for bad, the Reaction Control Center was activated, and area-wide contingency plans were implemented at nine o'clock on that first morning of overt war in Georgia.

At twenty minutes past nine, the first of a series of lightning strikes by a "lone gunman" in and around the financial district of Atlanta provided the first test and initial failure of the police planning. By nine-thirty, the ranks of "the inner circle of crime bosses" in Atlanta had been decimated, with the slayings of five known syndicate "businessmen" as well as their personal bodyguards.

A frustrated watch commander at the RCC lamely explained to his superiors: "We simply weren't set up yet for that kind of reaction. We didn't get the first gunfire report until zero-nine-twenty-six hours. By then they were popping in from all over the district. We had Five Points sealed solid within minutes after that first report came down. And that goddamn guy was already out of it and gone."

The police planners went back to their drawing boards, muttering over the impossibility of instant reaction to an infinite spectrum of possible events.

Alluding to those same incidents, a shamed "security boss" reported in a telephone call to the mansion on Paces Ferry Road: "I don't know how he did it; he just did it. We had everything covered, just like we worked it out last night, and there was a Band-Aid tagman with every one of them. He took the tagmen, too. I never saw such a guy before. Where the hell is that hotshot bunch from New York, anyways? I can't cover all the shit this guy might decide to throw!"

A follow-up call, several minutes later, reported:

"He hit your Five Points office, too, sir! Cleaned out the vault and torched a whole lot of stuff. They're still going through the ashes, trying to— when? We don't know when. They found it like that when they opened up, at nine."

At precisely ten o'clock, young David Ecclefield was joined in his vehicle, just outside the Civil War Cyclorama in Grant Park, by a tall man wearing yellow eyeshades and a safari-style leisure suit. The precise time and point of the meeting had been established moments earlier via cryptic directions over an Atlanta police radio channel.

"Let's move," the visitor suggested as he slid in beside the Federal cop.

They moved instantly, cruising slowly out of the park and along Southeast Boulevard.

Bolan placed a briefcase on the backseat as he explained to his companion, "There's some ammunition for your war. Don't ask where or how I got it, and I won't tell you anything to ruffle your official sensibilities. One more link to the chain, and you can topple the Sciaparelli empire—all nice and legal. You'll need the Walters books, and I don't know where to tell you to look for them. Later, maybe."

Ecclefield was eyeing the guy as much as he could risk without appearing overly fascinated. The cop's palms were clammy on the steering wheel and his voice a bit ragged as he inquired, "What's in the briefcase?"

"Financial codes, I'd guess. The keys to the Walters books. Here's something you need to know. The clean books sort of caught fire awhile ago. They no longer exist. So his people will have a hell of a time reconstructing them because they were all lies and manipulations. If you can bust him quick on the Walters data, lock up everything, and keep it legally frozen, they'll go crazy trying to refute your case."

"That's stupendous," admitted the strike-force boss. "I already have some people working the Walters angle. I've established a legal framework, anyway. What, uh, where have you been the past hour?"

"Don't ask," Bolan suggested.

"Okay, I won't. But I just heard some amazing stuff on the radio. Five Points got blitzed about half an hour ago."

"Imagine that," Bolan said lightly.

"You're a mighty tough man, Mr.—I'm sorry, you never identified yourself, did you?"

"Some people in your line of work call me Striker."

"That's very fitting. It could even fit me, couldn't it?"

Bolan gave the guy a sober grin, a mere flash of white teeth. "I told you, Ecclefield, that we're in the same business. Our difference is largely a point of view."

"Our difference," the youngster argued, "is largely one of effectiveness. I envy your freedom but not your peril. What can I do for you, Striker?"

"You can wreck the Sciaparelli empire for me, Ecclefield. I can make heads roll, yeah, if you call that effectiveness. But this is a monster that grows new heads as fast as you whack them off. I can't reach the roots, guy. You can. Do it."

"I'll give it my damndest," the Fed replied soberly. "I guess I am more of a roots-and-tangle man—not a head whacker, like you. But I suspect that you make it sound far too simple, for yourself. It's more complex than that, isn't it? The head-whacking. What is it that really burns your guts, Striker?"

"It's the rot that burns my guts, David. It's dreams dashed, lives wasted, and decent men corrupted in wholesale lots that burns my guts. It's a system that dehumanizes and brutalizes everything it touches that burns my guts. Shall I go on?"

"I get the idea," the Fed replied, sighing. "I figured it that way. You're no soldier of fortune, mister."

"Never pretended to be."

"Sometimes the media play it that way. Sometimes they play it with you in the heavy role—the big bad psychopath with a God complex. I never could buy either version. I always had you figured as a guy with a burn he couldn't put out, a guy with a heart too damned big to live and let live on a sinking ship."

"Thanks for the vote," Bolan said quietly. "You can drop me now—back where we started."

"Okay. But when you called, you mentioned an exchange of intelligence. So far it's been a one-way street. What can I give you in exchange?"

"Maybe you've already given it."

"I can give you more than votes, mister. Try me."

"When the time comes, David, I promise to try you."

"Okay. I'll be around."

They drove on in silence for a moment. Then Ecclefield told the big guy, "I talked to Brognola, by the way."

"Congratulations."

"I've heard whispers about that guy."

"Not from me."

The young Fed sighed. "Not from you, right." He sighed again and drummed his fingers on the steering wheel. "Some day, Mister Striker, I hope to join the fraternity."

"You already have, guy. Once you start living large, there's no avenue of retreat. This is good—drop me here."

The cop pulled over, and the tall man got out.

He leaned back inside to say, "Stay hard, friend." Then he closed the door and walked quickly away, disappearing immediately in the greenery.

"Stay what?" the cop muttered to himself.

He got the meaning, though.

And, yeah, he'd damn sure found himself a friend—perhaps, he mused, an entire fraternity of friends.

10: Brothers

It was just past ten o'clock when the caravan reappeared at the mansion on Paces Ferry Road. Mellini had seen them cruise past once, moving slowly and eyeballing the layout. Apparently, they'd made a complete circle to approach from the same direction again.

Five cars, loaded for head, were moving like a funeral procession at car-length separation, halting now, looking, and now nosing cautiously into the circular drive.

Mellini popped a fist into a palm and paced the porch. *Come on, dammit! This is it! Come on!*

The lead vehicle had barely entered the grounds when doors popped open to disgorge four quickly moving men who ran on ahead while the creeping caravan inched forward.

Well, Jesus Christ at breakfast! Talk about skittery!

A tense and jittery house boss danced halfway down the stairs to greet the runners, shouting to them: "What the hell are you doing! Get it on in here!"

A frozen-faced headhunter tossed him a cool glance and gave a hand signal to call the vehicles on.

Two of the runners circled to the rear of the house. The other two proceeded on along the drive toward the far end.

Mellini the Mick had never seen anything like this before. What did those guys think they had there?—a Presidential cavalcade, for Chrissakes!

The caravan picked up speed and then formed a wedge as the cars squealed to a halt beneath the portico. All doors opened at once, and the debarkation onto this strange turf was accomplished en masse. That mass split immediately, though, with two men jogging up the steps past Mellini without so much as a nod and other small groups moving off across those grounds like a slow-motion explosion of holiday fireworks.

A tight knot of them remained at the bottom of the stairs, quietly looking the situation over.

The house boss found his voice again to announce to that latter group, "I saw you guys cruise past. Didn't you hear me yelling? Where the hell have you been all this time? Christ! Frankie said—"

"Who are you?"

The inquiry came from a cool-eyed dude who'd moved from the center of the group.

"I'm Mellini."

The house boss had possibly been entertaining an exaggerated sense of his own fame—since that last visitor. The fall came cruelly.

"What's a Mellini?"

"Uh . . . I'm the head cock. Where the hell have you people been? Frankie said you were coming right along. We're thin as spring ice around here. And that damn guy has been running wild all over town."

The cool dude was moving up the steps.

"Who is Frankie?"

"What d'you mean, who is Frankie! Aren't you guys—"

Mellini the Head Cock found himself staring at another black playing card.

"Domino," the guy announced coldly. "Who is Frankie?"

This was all very confusing, much too confusing for a guy who had been at the ragged edge of hysteria for going on ten hours now.

Mellini growled, "Aw, shit."

"Tell your boss I'm here."

Sciaparelli stepped onto the porch to say, "His boss already knows you're here. And he's glad you're here. Come on in."

Domino introduced his carbons. "This is Paul. This is James. And this is John."

Mellini muttered, but no one heard, "And I suppose you're Jesus."

"Sciaparelli. Call me Ship; all my friends do. Come in, come in. First time in Atlanta? Too bad it has to be this way."

The party was flowing across the porch and into the house. The two men who had first ascended the steps remained outside, pulling the door closed behind the party.

Mellini was growing more and more uncomfortable about the whole thing. He took his boss by the arm and savagely whispered, "Something's haywire! Let's check it out!"

Sciaparelli turned to Domino with a bland smile. "Just to keep it square, let's see your marks, eh."

Domino handed over an I.D. wallet.

They all went into the study.

Sciaparelli took his chair at the desk and picked up the telephone.

The others silently took places around the table as the boss of Atlanta made his verification call to the New York headshed.

The conversation was very brief. Sciaparelli read something from the backside of the playing card then scratched his cheek as the receiver rattled at his ear.

"So who is Frankie?" he asked solemnly.

The receiver rattled again.

He said, "Never mind, we'll handle it," and hung up.

He returned the wallet to the Black Ace and asked him, "Who is Frankie?"

The guy shrugged and put the wallet away. "There are many Frankies, Ship."

"He was flashing a card just like yours. He came in here and took the place over. And he waltzed out of here with a very sensitive project."

"When was all this?"

The Ship's eyes flicked to the clock. "Maybe five hours ago. He supposedly brought a crew with him

... like yours. They never showed. We were beginning to wonder."

"You didn't check him out?"

Sciaparelli asked, "How often do you get checked out, Domino?"

The guy spread his hands and smiled. "Tell me how he looked."

"Big guy. Football shoulders, ballet hips. Cool and commanding. Dressed in a . . . what?—sports suit? Tan—beige, I guess. Hunting-style coat. Yellow shades on the eyes."

Domino's gaze shot to the lieutenant at his left hand. The other guy cocked his head about a millimeter and returned the gaze.

Mellini's voice cracked as he cried, "Aw, hell no! It couldn't be!"

"Yes it could," Domino said, still locked in that gaze with his lieutenant. "The guy is solid class. He'd try it. We've been wondering about some of his past—that's it, James. We make a note to table this when we get back. John? Paul? Make the note. Bolan has been masquerading as a Black Ace. We have to plug that when we get back if it falls to hell here."

No one responded, except with the eyes.

Mellini sputtered, "I still don't believe it."

"Start believing," Domino purred. "There's another crack somewhere, too, very high in the woodwork. We were met."

Sciaparelli said, "What?"

"He was waiting at the airport. Same guy."

"When was that?"

"We landed at six."

"That was four hours ago!"

Mellini howled, "What d'you mean, he met you!"

No one dignified that outburst with a direct reply. Domino was staring at Sciaparelli as he explained, "The hotshot tossed a legion of cops at us. We've been all this time getting clear."

"How'd he do that?" Sciaparelli asked, awed.

"How did he take you over, Ship?"

"It's scary," the house boss muttered. "Spooky."

"Maybe you didn't hear," Sciaparelli told Domino. "The guy tore through my downtown territory about an hour ago. He took five of my *caporegimes* with him. They all had bodyguards. They all died. I'm glad you're here. Frankly, it's out of my league, and I'm not ashamed to say it. I don't care if you have to burn Atlanta again; I want that guy out of my hair. These aren't just my interests, you know. All the men who sent you have investments here. I'm glad you're here. My home is yours. My town is yours. Stop the guy."

Sciaparelli got to his feet and strode from the room.

Mellini rose to follow him.

Domino purred, "Stay, head cock."

Mellini stayed.

"Frankie, eh?"

"That's what he said I could call him."

One of the carbons quietly snickered.

"Okay, I should've known better, sure, but I didn't. He even fooled Ship. I mean, he actually backed Ship down on a point dear to Ship's heart. But I guess I should've . . ."

"Don't feel bad," Domino said smoothly. "He fooled me, too. I pegged him as an undercover Fed playing cute games. Okay. That's all in the past.

We're working toward the future now. Tell me everything you know about our friend Frankie, head cock."

Mellini was sweating, despite the forgiving words and soothing tone. These guys might bend him over a fire. They might pour salt down his throat and cement up his ass. And who would say nay to them? Ship had just handed them his town.

These supercocks from New York were not like the *amici*. Hell no. These supercocks were killer robots, programmed for one all-consuming mission. That mission was to protect and preserve the federation against its enemies—and against itself, even, should that need arise.

They were not Mellini the Mick's friends, hell no, and not even the boss of Atlanta's friends.

Not these guys.

They were the devil's disciples, that's what they were—James and John notwithstanding.

They lived for one thing now—Mack Bolan's head. They intended to deliver it to the old men in New York—not to Ship, hell no.

And it wouldn't matter to them how many other heads they wasted along the way.

Mellini cleared his throat and tried to steady his voice as he told the devil's domino: "Hey, I want this guy as much as you do. I can close my eyes and see him right now—every little detail. I can describe the car he was driving when he left here, and I can even give you the license number. I have pictures of the broad he took with him, and I can tell you things about that doll to jiggle your eyeballs.

"You want patterns, shadings, marks—right?

Okay. So get comfortable. I'm going to give you . . ."

Yeah. Damned right. Mellini the Mick was going to give those guys everything they ever wanted.

They weren't *amici*, no. But they were, hell, his brothers—weren't they?

Confidentially, though, Mellini the Mick liked Frankie quite a bit better.

11: Soundings

Bolan was in his "warwagon," the specially equipped GMC motor home that served combination duty as battle cruiser, scout ship, and base camp. It was also the closest thing to a home the guy could claim. The big rig represented a six-figure investment—though it was paid for with enemy dollars from the war chest—and utilized the ultimate in space-age technology. (See: *New Orleans Knockout.*)

Optic and audio systems were activated as he rolled through the exclusive neighborhood in a pass on the Sciaparelli estate, recording the sights and sounds of the place as greatly magnified and enhanced by the sophisticated hardware.

He did not risk a second pass but continued on his course for the most direct connection to the interstate north, although his naked perceptions of the area had revealed nothing whatever of intelligence value. He had learned to trust the warwagon's surveillance capabilities, and he was confident that a reduction of the electronic data would disclose details that lay beyond ordinary human sensitivity.

He programmed the scans as he drove on northward, so that the intelligence was ready for his personal evaluation by the time he arrived in the vicinity of his base camp on the southern shore of Allatoona Lake.

The warwagon's "slot" was directly across a small inlet from the rented fishing cabin. As a routine precaution, he focused the barrel pickups of the audio surveillance system on the cabin and set the system for manual monitoring while he analyzed the intelligence from the Sciaparelli scans.

The ghostly mutterings coming through the audio monitors were buried in a background cacophony of magnified sounds contributed by everything from insects to sighing winds to distant engine noises. Bolan refined the focus, resolving the mutterings to the deep-well echoes of human voices.

There was no intent to eavesdrop on his new friends.

The intent was pure military caution, born of harsh experience in such matters. The situation appeared normal over there, however. The Georgia Cowboy and Miss Superskate seemed to be hitting if off okay, too, after that initially tense confrontation when Bolan first brought them eye to eye.

The cowboy's voice came through the barrels as a deep rumble. "Guess I'm getting my third wind, or maybe it's the fourth. Not even sleepy, anymore. But my stomach ... God!"

The superskate came across like a talking doll: "I could make some sandwiches. Or I see he has some canned soup, too."

"Oh naw, naw—thanks. Let's go through it again. You say Shorty came out to the house last Tuesday. Take it again from there."

"I'm sick of this, just sick of it!"

Bolan grinned and diffused the scan, consigning that conversation once again to the realm of ghostly mutterings. He went to work immediately on the intelligence readings. The video resolutions were quite good, but the audio yielded very little. He found a man on the roof and another in the bushes near the road, several more on foot patrols around the grounds. One face showed up remarkably clear at an upstairs window. It looked, at first, like Jennifer Rossiter but he knew that could not be so—deciding that it was Jennifer's sister, Suzy Sciaparelli. There was a haunting quality to that face. Bolan sighed regretfully and continued his evaluation of the data. The full job required about ten minutes. Then he secured the systems, activated the electronic safeguards, and went to join his friends at the "cover" base.

The mission problems, as Bolan saw them, were both varied and confusing. There had been an escalation, of sorts, to this Georgia war. His primary goal, when first he descended upon this Southern stronghold, had been to harass and disrupt their trade lanes. He'd come in with heroin from Mexico and quickly found himself confronted with a billion-dollar annual traffic in other unlawful commodities, as well. Sciaparelli himself was a large question mark. The guy had no pedigree whatever that Bolan could discern. He neither was among the old men nor was he ranked with the young turks. Who and what was he, then, and from where had he sprung?

The usual sources of information had yielded very little on the guy. He had been the subject of a couple of quiet Federal investigations: nothing handed down, no indictments, not even a grand-jury subpoena. He was thought to have had links with Vannaducci of New Orleans but there was no hard link between the two. A reporter for *The Atlanta Constitution* had written a series of articles recently, regarding the "Dixie Mafia" in which Sciaparelli's name was bandied about with frequent use of the cautious adjectives "alleged" and "purported." The guy had no criminal record whatever, not even a traffic citation, and there was absolutely nothing in his past to tie him directly to a mob sponsorship.

And yet there was no doubt whatever that Charles Sciaparelli was the Mafia boss of Atlanta and surrounding regions.

The only clue to the pedigree was buried in the "business" background of the guy. He had a degree from Columbia, credentials with the New York Stock Exchange, and had once managed a large portfolio of investments for a syndicate cover group. But where did the pedigree begin? Couldn't it have pre-dated the Columbia years, even? The mob had educated a number of fair-haired boys to finesse their complicated stratagems in the straight world—converting dirty money to clean and back to dirty again.

The New York mobs had been undergoing quite an evolution in recent years, with much unrest and shuffling about within and across family lines. Bolan himself had contributed rather dramatically to that unrest. Somewhere in there, in that confused and sometimes chaotic evolution of criminal empire, the boss of Atlanta had been born. Whole cloth, as it were.

Bolan suspected that the guy was nothing but a cover for one of the old men in New York—Marinello, perhaps, or one of the other more powerful *capos*—an open con on the other bosses, the extension of personal domain beyond normal boundaries. It was not an unlikely situation; it had been done before, many times. The intriguing aspect of all that, of course, was that the other bosses always knew they were being conned; by unspoken agreement, they were party to their own victimization at the hands of one of their peers. It was a funny world, this world of Mafia. The guys played games with themselves, curious games of deceit and intrigue, all the while proclaiming the sanctity of honor and brotherhood. Occasionally, one of them went too far, and he was either gently tapped back into line or blasted completely out of that curious world. It had happened time and again. The Sciaparelli "question" therefore loomed large in Bolan's combat sensitivities.

Ecclefield had been absolutely correct in his assessment of the Bolan "motivational package." It was no simple contest between casual head whackers. Mack Bolan's very soul was committed to the contest; for this warrior, it was a question of who would operate the world: men or savages. It was not a political question nor even a moral one, and his war was certainly not a hate fest—not from Bolan's point of view, anyway. In his understanding, it was the most important war ever fought by anyone, anywhere—and it was therefore to be waged in the pure realms of extinction and survival. He could not afford to overlook any weapon, any stratagem, or any device that may turn the world toward an extinction of savages and the survival of men.

Not simple, no.

And Mack Bolan was not a simple man.

The lady was giving him a rather awed inspection as he removed his coat and came out of the gun-leather.

"Grover has been telling tales out of school," she reported breathlessly.

Bolan grinned as he replied, "All to the point, I hope."

The cowboy chuckled. "I'm an amateur general, you know. Been following your campaigns for a long time." He shrugged. "She asked. I told her, between rounds."

"What have you developed concerning our late little buddy?"

The girl and the cowboy locked eyes for a moment, then the guy laughed a bit self-consciously and said, "Well let's cover the sensitive points first. Number one, they were not lovers. Number two, she did everything in her power to influence him away from Sciaparelli, not toward him. Number three, anyone who says she ever drove around totally naked in the superskate is a damned liar. She is not that stupid, that depraved, or that desperate for attention. Number four, I now fully accept the truth of points one, two, and three."

Bolan's comment to that was couched in the tones of a man who had been there himself. "Well, sometimes reputations are conceived in optimism, born of hope, and fed by unusual expectation. Are you sure about point three, though?"

Reynolds chuckled and replied, "I guess so, dammit."

The lady complained, "Quit talking about me as though I'm not here." The eyes crackled at the cowboy. "And I can take care of my own defense."

"Just squaring the record," Reynolds said lightly. He asked Bolan, "What's going down?"

"Plenty," Bolan growled. He grabbed the girl and hugged her roughly. Then he set her down and went to the bathroom to wash up.

Jennifer dropped dizzily into a chair, a hand at her forehead, and Reynolds leaned in the open doorway to talk as Bolan scrubbed.

"I'm beginning to feel like a cop again—even thinking like one. Listen—I've had to revise my image of Shorty, not that I don't still think of him warmly. He's still like a lost brother. But that little shit was into some heavy stuff, I think."

"Glad you discovered it first," Bolan replied. "I suspected as much from the beginning."

"I should have," the cowboy quietly admitted. "That was a pretty good trick, sending me back along the trails and having me re-examine the tracks. I was already looking at the pattern with a clearer eye when Jenny convinced me that Shorty had been working her for information."

"We were pals," she called faintly from the kitchen.

"Road buddies," Reynolds explained. "They met at a spontaneous coffee freak—you know, a CB clutch. Twenty or so breakers congregated on the place, and Shorty was one of them. It went from that to trips in the cab on short hauls."

"Just for fun, not for frolic," the lady elaborated.

Reynolds continued, "Apparently he'd made some connection between Sciaparelli and Bluebird. He kept asking Jenny about family connections and business interests. Last Tuesday, he went out to her house and busted in on Sciaparelli. Jenny says they had a long talk, and Shorty went away very happy."

"Shakedown, maybe?"

"Yeah, maybe. It sort of points that way. I don't see how he could have scored any other connection."

Bolan draped a towel about his shoulders and turned to the cowboy with a troubled face. "Was Shorty an ex-cop, too?" he asked quietly.

"Yeah. I thought I told you that. We served together. But then I went to 'Nam, and he didn't. When I got back, he was driving truck. That left only Billy Bob."

"Who is Billy Bob?"

"The third leg of the three musketeers. We went through school together, the three of us—played ball together, went on the Cobb force together. I guess Billy Bob was the only true cop, though. He's still with the force."

"Still friends?"

"Sure. We bowled together, my last home stand. That's rare, though. He moonlights another job, and I'm on the road most of the time. But we're still close. Why? Are you thinking, maybe, of a connection?"

Bolan shrugged. "Something to keep in mind, maybe. An eye or an ear on the inside never hurts. For now, I'd say let's keep the club as exclusive as possible. I already have a contact."

The lady said, "Hey, guys."

Bolan grinned at her. "Yeah?"

"I just wanted to make sure I'm still here."

"Did you have something to say?"

"I have plenty to say," the lady assured him.

"Try it, then."

"I've decided that Suzy will just have to lie in her own bed. I'm not sharing it with her any longer. I want to sing, Sergeant."

Bolan pulled up a chair, took both her hands, and told her, "It will have to be the prettiest sounds I've heard all day."

12: Keys

Jennifer Rossiter was the key to the Sciaparelli question, of course, and Bolan had known that all along. He had suspected also that she would come to him in her own time—and she had not disappointed him in that expectation.

Suzy was an older sister—but not that much older, and there was a considerable age difference between herself and her husband. After four years of marriage, though, she apparently remained "deeply fascinated" by the guy. Jennifer simply would not believe that her sister was "in love" with Sciaparelli.

"He's a pig," she said witheringly.

Fascination was a word that she could better accept for her sister, and it was just the opposite of her own reaction to the man. She was thoroughly repelled by him.

Suzy had been "behaving neurotically" for the past couple of years—"torn between the louse and sanity." There were moments when she seemed to despise her husband, but she flew into a defensive rage any time Jennifer suggested a termination of the marriage. For the past year, Jennifer had been living with the Sciaparellis. Why? "Just to keep Suzy sane. I thought I could give her something he couldn't—tears and sympathy, if nothing else. But I'm sick of it. Believe me, after two days of house arrest, I am sick to death of it."

From Jennifer's own observations and from her awareness of household routines and influences, as well as from conversations with her sister, the young lady knew quite a lot about Charles Sciaparelli.

As she unloaded it on Bolan—at times in response to direct questions but generally as a torrential release—he was pleased to discover that most of the keys were there.

Coupled to his own understanding of the complex interactions within the world of Mafia, and that coupled again to a simple extension of logic, Bolan was able to draw a rather accurate three-dimensional picture of the Georgia empire as well as the forces behind it.

When she had finally wrung herself dry on the subject, Bolan asked the lady, "Why were you under house arrest?"

"I thought that was obvious. He wanted me to tell him about Shorty. All I gave him was name, rank, and serial number. He kept hinting that there was some dark plot, that someone was out to get him, and that I was mixed up in it, knowingly or unknowingly. I thought he was just trying to trap me into saying something dumb about Shorty. I actually did not know what was going on. So I told him nothing. So he said I could just stay in my room until I decided to cooperate. So I took off my clothes and dared any of them to walk through that door again."

Bolan chuckled. "Did it work?"

"Most of the time."

"And, when it didn't?"

She raised those lovely arms and dropped them. "I just kept my eyes closed and my mouth screaming until they left."

"You didn't scream when I came in."

"It was dumb. I got tired of it."

"You say they locked you up two days ago?"

"Yes. This would have been the third day."

Bolan looked at Reynolds. "Where was Shorty two days ago, cowboy?"

"With me on the flip-flop from Detroit. We just got back yesterday."

Okay. That figured. The guy was on the road when Ship, or someone, decided to take him.

"Ship put Jenny on ice," Bolan muttered.

She said, "What?"

"I don't believe he meant to hurt you. Just the opposite. I believe he was protecting you."

The lady was giving him a troubled look.

Reynolds said, "He was trying to keep her out of play. Shorty was already a marked man."

"He marked himself," Bolan growled. "He tried the wrong combination. He caught somebody by the short hairs."

"Sciaparelli, sure."

"Maybe. Maybe not. What kind of shakedown could the guy hope to pull off? Look who he was tackling. He must have known he couldn't hope to hack something like that. Could an ex-cop be that naive?"

"So what do you think?" the cowboy mused.

"I don't know. It'll have to roll around inside the skull for a while until something settles into place. I'm getting a feeling, though. I believe Ship was expecting somebody down from New York before I ever touched him. I believe he was dreading it. I stared the guy down this morning when I took Jenny out of there. He really shouldn't have backed off that way, considering the circumstances. It was the act of a threatened man—a vulnerable man. It sure wasn't . . ."

Something was shuttling back and forth across Bolan's inner vision—some picture, fighting for resolution.

"What's wrong?" Reynolds asked.

"Nothing's wrong. It's getting right, now. Jenny?"

"Yes, sir," she replied soberly.

"Was it your idea that you move in with your sister and her husband?"

"Gosh, no. I told you. I did it for Suzy's sake."

"She asked you."

"She drove me crazy for a week. I finally gave in."

"Where's your family?"

"My mother died two years ago."

"Your father?"

"When I was a little girl. I barely remember him."

"So you're all alone in the world."

"Except for Suzy."

"Except for Suzy," Bolan echoed.

The shuttling loom had found its resolution.

Bolan said, quietly, "Jenny—who is Henry?"

"Henry Jackson? He's an adorable old black man. He's my—my . . ."

"Your what?"

"Why are you looking at me like that?"

"It's important. Who is Henry?"

"Well, I don't know what to call it. I never thought about it. He's just Henry. Can a man be a housekeeper? Do girls have butlers? He's been with the family for years. I inherited him."

"Which family?"

"*My* family. After my mother died, he was the only family I had, except Suzy, and she was all knotted up with Charles. I was still in school. Henry stayed on and took care of things for me. Why? Has something happened to Henry?"

"Let's hope not. So he's your man, not Ship's."

"Right. He came along with me when I moved in a year ago. Charles took over the employer responsibilities. But he mainly took care of Suzy and me. Charles already had his own gun-toting footmen. What is this all about? Could Henry be in danger in that house? My God, Suzy's there. She wouldn't let—"

"I think it's okay," Bolan said quickly, heading off an emotional tizzy. "If Henry took my advice, and I'm sure he did, then he's long gone from Paces Ferry Road. Where do you think he would go?"

She blinked at that. "I have no idea. Back to my place, maybe."

"You still have a place?"

"Sure. In Decatur. What *is* this?"

"Keys, sweetie, just keys. Relax. Henry has been with the family a long time, eh."

"Since right after my father died."

"Your mother worked."

"No. She was not very healthy. I guess my father left us in pretty good shape financially. The house was paid for. There was always plenty of money. What kind of keys?"

"To the past, maybe," Bolan muttered.

He got up and strapped on the gun-leather. "I'll have to ask you two to stay buried a while longer. If I'm not back within a couple of hours, stop expecting me. You'll have to play it by ear from there."

"Hey, hold it!" Reynolds growled. "If it's all that tight, I want a piece of it."

"You already have a piece, and I'm going to need you for more urgent things; so save it. Jenny—I'd like to use your hot rod."

"Take it," she said quietly. "And bring it back— with *you* in it."

He grinned and told her, "I intend to."

"Just give me a hint," the cowboy worriedly insisted. "Maybe it's better than I'm thinking."

"Maybe it's not," Bolan replied grimly. "Stay with the odds, guy." He pulled him to the door and spoke softly for private hearing. "She could be hot as hell. If I don't get back, use my name and contact a guy named Ecclefield, strike force in Atlanta. Tell him to put the girl somewhere cool. He'll know what to do."

The guy was beginning to *look* like a cop. He replied, "Yeah, I have that. Take care, Big B."

"You, too," Bolan said, and cracked the door open.

The lady catapulted across the room in a sudden flying lunge, slamming the door and inserting herself between it and Bolan.

He said, "Hey!"

She said, "I checked you. I don't want it anonymous, not ever again. Give me something to hold until you get back."

He took her in his arms and kissed her, long and tender, then asked her, "Something like that?"

"Just like that," she said, and made a run for the bathroom.

Reynolds smiled and commented, "Well, there's something to grow on."

"Or die with," Bolan muttered, and went out of there.

Keys, yeah, the girl held the keys.

And what a curious place was this Mafia world.

Bolan went first to the warwagon and fired up the data console, found frustration there, then risked the mobile phone for a combination to Pittsfield. He had to run it three times before Turrin came on the line, and the guy was sounding just a bit on the ragged edge.

"This is La Mancha. Are you clean, Leo?"

"Yeh, it's clean. Jesus Christ, where have you been? I've been trying to turn you all day."

"I've been off the floater, Leo—just got back. What's all the huff?"

"Hell, I think the world's about to stop and let everyone off. I think maybe I'm in deep shit, Sarge. Listen, I'm going to be fading off for a while. I already got the wife and kids packed away."

"What is it, Leo?"

"It's heat, Sarge, and it's moving my way."

"I should be clear by tomorrow," Bolan said quickly. "Find a low spot and stay put. Keep hitting my floater so I'll know where. Have you alerted Hal?"

"Yeh, he knows but I'm not going along with his fix. It would blow everything for good. There's still a chance here, and I think it's worth trying for."

"Just keep it covered, buddy. We'll work it together."

"Thanks, big guy. I was hoping you'd say something like that. Okay. I'm going to tough it through. I'll hit you every even hour from now on until we contact again. Uh . . . how're things in ax-handle acres?"

"Same as everywhere, Leo. Do you have a minute for a quickie?"

"Yeh. Try me."

"When I talked to Hal this morning, he said you'd sent the alert on the head party."

"Yeh, right. I couldn't turn you. He said he passed it."

"I got it, yeah. What I'm wondering, now . . . when did you send that word, Leo? Before or after you got my fix?"

"Right about the same time, I guess. I was on the phone with the headshed when your thing came down. I mean, I got it right off the ticker. The guy passes it on to me as it's coming in. And he says something like it's going to be a hot time in Atlanta because the Domino and his crew are heading that way."

"That's the way he put it, eh? Which should mean that the Domino was already sent—shouldn't it?"

"Well, no—well, yeah, maybe so. I didn't put it together that way, but—yeah, I guess so. Unless Domino was sitting there just waiting for your thing to go down, because I got it before he did."

"Okay, Leo, it fits. Thanks, guy. Hey, you cover it. I'll be there. That's a promise."

"So will I. And that's another promise."

Bolan popped the connection and immediately tried another combination, this one to Washington.

He got it the first time, and said, "This is Striker. Clear me."

He sat through the usual rundown of clicks and squeals, then Brognola told him, "Okay, it's clear. What's happening?"

"I just talked to Sticker."

"I hope you talked some sense into him."

"Yeah, I agreed that he should cool it and tough it. I'll be up there tomorrow."

"Fine. That's all I need. I'll be running naked through the streets of Washington tomorrow, Striker."

"Maybe no. What's moving on the Sticker?"

"It smells like a general purge, buddy. Things are very tense in New York. The explosion threatens to reach all the way to our buddy. Sticker might lose a sponsor—and you know what that means."

Bolan said, "Yeah. Okay. It all fits. I think maybe it's reaching here, too, Hal. I don't have time to give you details but something is definitely rumbling, and I believe it started before I got here. I'm on short time, so I want you to give me something right off your head—don't go pulling files or anything. I'm going back now to a time when Jake Pelotti was an underboss under Saranghetti, New York City, more than fifteen years ago.

"Okay. Go ahead."

"A guy went for a hit on Jake a few days before his elevation to *capo*."

"Right. But the guy botched it. Jake picked up a flesh wound and went into hiding until his boys could safe it for him."

"Okay. Who was that hit man, Hal?"

"Oh, hell. We're going back a long way, Striker, and still nobody knows for sure. A few chunks of a human body floated up in the East River a few days after that hit, enough left of it for fingerprint indentification. It was generally felt that this was the hit man, but that was never actually established. He was a free-lancer."

"I have that. I'm going for a name, Hal."

"Shame on you. How could you forget a name like that one?"

"Let's have it."

"Uh, a very peculiar—yeah. James. John Paul James."

"That's a positive?"

"It is. Right off the head, Striker."

"Okay, thanks. I'm sure I have him in my files, but all I could get was a picture, a news clipping or something, I don't know. I'll find it. And, Hal, give the Sticker all the cover you can, huh?"

"Now look who's worrying."

"Not us—right?"

"Right. Not us."

Bolan killed the combination and turned immediately to his data console. A picture, yeah. For some reason, it had flashed on him as he was talking with Jennifer Rossiter, but nothing else would come from it. Some subliminally recorded image, no doubt—something adhering to the gray tissues from a routine data scan—but it was in the files somewhere, and it had to do with Jake Pelotti, the current head of a New York family.

It was not banked under Pelotti—he'd already checked that. But, yeah, there it was under James, John Paul.

It was a microfilm transparency lifted from an old newspaper clipping. It was a photo of a smiling man and woman and two little girls, snapshot quality and dimmed with age long before the microfilm was made.

The faces were hardly distinguishable, but that did not really matter.

It was the caption that mattered.

Suspected Victims of Gangland Retaliation. John P. James, his wife, Elizabeth, daughters Susan and Jennifer.

Yeah.
It was a hell of a key.

13: Strongheart

Bolan knew what he had to do. That was not the question. The question was *how* to do it. And, of course, the answer was obvious, simple, and scary. There was only one way to do it. A bit of engineering, perhaps, could make it slide a bit slicker. But all chutes led to the one inescapable end.

He had to make a daylight penetration of the Sciaparelli household, and he had to do it with all cute tricks inoperative.

He had to go in there cold against a professional force of headhunters.

Unless ...

"Try me," the guy had offered.

Bolan got the guy on the horn and reminded him.

"Sure. The invitation is still open," the young Fed assured him.

"Okay. Don't ask any questions you don't want the answers to. And don't waltz me around—this one is purely for marbles, so just say yes or no. I need an official presence, in force, at the Sciaparelli home, exactly one hour from now."

"*Exactly* one hour?"

"Yeah. My watch says it's seven past the hour . . . right . . . now."

"Check. You'll have it. Wouldn't it help if I knew a little about the game plan?"

"It could keep you up nights, friend. How's the paper work going?"

"Smashingly," the guy replied, a pleased ring to the voice. "I've already moved for that lockup you suggested. Preliminary indications are for complete approval within the hour."

"You do move fast," Bolan complimented him.

"I have fast friends," the cop replied with a chuckle. "At seven past the hour. Okay. We have a date."

Bolan said, "You won't be seeing me, friend, I hope."

"What am I supposed to be doing?"

"It should look like a gentle bust—soft and easy, nothing big, but with plenty of presence. You could run into a hot lead curtain damn quick unless you finesse it."

"I'm going in to serve papers, or something."

"Something like that, yeah. But you're taking your force along, just in case."

"I have it. I'm going to be a very diverting fellow."

Bolan chuckled solemnly. "Yeah, you have it. I'll need, at minimum, five minutes of presence from the time you hit the property."

"You'll get it, Striker. Rely on it."

Bolan left the guy on that note and began his preparations for a daylight strike into hard territory.

Diversionary force or not, it was not going to be easy. Ease, of course, was not the name of the game.

The name of the game was *war against the Mafia*—to the very bitter end.

Indeed ... to the final faltering heartbeat.

Bolan was in faded blue denims, chambray shirt, dungaree jacket—black, featherlight sneakers on the feet. He wore the .44 thunderpiece at the right hip and lashed to the leg. Whispering death rode the shoulder harness. A few accessories occupied a small belt pouch at the belly.

He was poised and ready for a soft penetration of a very hard territory. The surrounding vegetation had helped but not much. He had allowed himself twenty minutes of quiet approach, and it had required every second of that. It was not that there were so many patrols; it was simply that what was there was so effectively positioned.

In addition to the guy on the roof, who had 360-degree surveillance capability, the rear approaches were controlled by a triangulation of outlooks that commanded the entire turf from three isolated posts. The apex of that triangle was farthest from the house. Behind that was some pretty wild country, densely thicketed, hilly terrain, sloping away to the rear with dry gulches and winding ravines. The two posts marking the base of the triangle were positioned just inside the cultivated "lawn" area. From that point on to the house, a distance of some sixty yards, it was no-man's land—totally open, no trees, patchworks of lawn and garden, patio and pool area, a couple of small utility buildings.

The sentries had walkie-talkies and shotguns, and each was in constant view of the other.

In a way, that made it nice for Bolan; he could keep them all in sight himself. At the other side of things, though, it was going to require some damn fancy footwork and precise timing to breach that defense.

And, then, there was that final problem.

Where the hell was the kicker?

These people always used one. The guys up on the outlooks were so much staked meat, waiting for a hit. They were not headmen and they would not be aware of that aspect of the game unless they had survived other sets such as this. Somewhere down there in that sprawl of lawn and gardens lurked a headhunter with an unrestricted view of all three outlooks plus the approaches to the house, like a spider poised at the top of a web, waiting for some unwary customer to come and nibble at the meat stakes.

Easy, no. Simple, no. It was a game for professional gladiators, and Bolan was thankful that he'd earned his stripes in the jungles of survival.

Thankful, yeah, because he'd finally spotted the guy.

It was no more than a flicker, a shadow movement as the guy shifted cramped limbs toward a more comfortable position, but Bolan caught it.

The kick man was in a cabana at the far side of the pool. The sun was west, and the open doorway was east toward Bolan. It was a perfect drop, difficult to see into because of the lighting situation, on high ground and commanding all rear approaches to the house.

Bolan sighed and checked the time.

It was six minutes past the hour.

He made a quick decision to go for meat. Any other move would subject him to an immediate crossfire and, if nothing worse, they could pin him flat and wait for reinforcements.

So, it was to be meat. He selected the target most distant from his position and took a quick range reading, mentally translating that to a ballistics course for the Beretta. The silencer complicated things at such a range, because so much muzzle velocity was lost to the sound-suppressing function.

Nevertheless, he would go with the Beretta and the whispering attack.

Wind was no factor. Trajectory drop, though, would be critical. Range velocity would fall sharply; he could not even depend on a knockdown without hitting a vital spot.

Trick-shot time again, yeah.

The trick-shot specialist took it from the prone and a two-hand hold, further steadying the firing platform atop a smooth rock and "holding over" the target a full two feet. He took a breath and released it slowly, squeezing with the sigh. The Beretta Belle whispered her soft note as she spat the Parabellum hi-shocker onto that difficult course.

Seventy yards downrange, the meat stake dropped everything and grabbed his belly, sinking to his knees and crying out with a frightened shriek: "I'm hit!"

The guy at twenty yards let out a grunt and

whirled toward that with his shotgun at the ready. The guy must have been at top tension for a long time. The piece *ba-loomed* in sheer reflex, adding to the unhappy circumstances of his fallen buddy.

The guy up at the apex yelled, "No, Harry! There's nothing in sight back here!" He was off his post and running toward the house.

Bolan was up and moving himself, taking full advantage of that heartbeat's worth of confusion. He danced into a garden stand of high sunflowers and dived behind a mound of fertilizer, as the kicker thrust a muzzle through the doorway of the cabana and laid on him with a burp gun.

Powdered manure and heavy sludge sucked up that first burst. And the kick man would not get off his second kick. The guy with the tense shotgun had whirled back at the first sound of chattering gunfire and emptied his magazine at that disturbance as fast as he could jerk the trigger.

It did not require a marksman for effectiveness with a shotgun. And, although the choke was undoubtedly a bit wide for that range, three quick charges of spraying pellets could saturate any target zone in a rather demoralizing manner—even for an in-the-know kicker.

The burp gun clattered to the tiles beside the pool as the headhunter sprouted multiple leaks and staggered into the open, hands at his face and pumping blood everywhere. He screamed, "You crazy! . . ." and tumbled into the water.

It was poetic, in a way, but Bolan had no time to appreciate the poetry of the turnabout. A heartbeat was all he'd asked for, and it was likely to be all he would get. He came to one knee with the thunderpiece at full extension and bellowing.

Two hundred and forty grains of splattering death reached out to touch first the stunned gunner with the runaway trigger finger and then the rear man, who realized too late that he was running in the wrong direction.

The rear was clear.

And the roofman had not shown himself since shortly before the shooting began.

As Bolan jogged past the cabana, he received a possible explanation for that. A walkie-talkie positioned just inside the door was squawking the urgent message: "Cease fire; cease fire! We got Feds here! All you boys stand down and be cool; be cool!"

The time was seven minutes and five seconds past the hour.

A heartbeat, yeah.

It was enough.

She'd gone to the window as soon as the shooting started, but she could see nothing except a line of cars trying to get into the drive and several of Mr. Domino's men flitting about the grounds.

A group of other men seemed to be blocking the drive, preventing entry of the cars.

A nice-looking younger man with a briefcase had stepped out of the first vehicle and was talking something over with the guards.

The gunfire seemed to be confusing everyone, even the men in the cars. Several of them had stepped to the street and were gazing warily about, their own guns coming into view. The man with the briefcase turned back to shout something. The men in the street returned to their cars.

The shooting was over.

One of Charles's men was walking rapidly down the drive, loudly explaining, "It's okay! Nervous guards! They thought it was something else!"

The cars were moving toward the house now.

She heard a sound at her door and whirled about to see a large man in denims standing in the open doorway. He was quite a remarkable-looking man and armed to the teeth. The face was coldly ferocious, but the voice was incredibly soft as he told her, "Don't be frightened, Suzy. I've come to take you to Jenny."

She said, "I haven't left this room for two years. I can't leave."

"Why not?"

She said, "Come here and I'll show you why not."

The man seemed hesitant, a bit tense. He cocked his head as though listening for something, then came into the room and closed the door.

"Over here," she said.

He joined her near the window and took both her hands. "This is life and death," he told her. "We have to go."

"Do you know Mr. Domino?"

He replied, "In a way, yeah."

She pointed to the men in the yard, below the window. They were grouped around the young man with the briefcase. Charles appeared from the portico and walked toward the group.

"Do you see Mr. Domino?"

"I see him. Come on, Suzy."

He was gently tugging at her.

She resisted. "The three men standing behind

Mr. Domino. They are John, Paul, and James. Isn't that queer?"

Her visitor quietly told her, "I know all about John Paul James. Let's go!"

She stamped her foot and told him, "Then you *must* know why I must not leave this room!"

"Are you going to stay here the rest of your life, Suzy?"

"I suppose so," she sadly replied.

She saw the fist coming, but not quite in time. She did not feel the blow, only numbness and a sudden weakness. She knew the sensation of floating weightless in space, and then she realized with a vague sort of understanding that she was hanging upside-down.

She was draped over the man's shoulder.

He was carrying her, taking her, taking her away!

She tried to scream, but nothing happened. It was another horrible nightmare! She relaxed. Soon she would awaken. Yes. She had learned how to defeat these awful dreams.

The dream continued, though, and she was moving along the hallway.

She saw two upside-down men appear at the head of the stairs. Something spun her as something else streaked very closely across her fogged vision—a hand, maybe.

Then, something sounded like *poof*, *poof*—and the upside-down men dived backward along the upside-down stairway.

She was moving through Jenny's room now. She floated through an open window, along the side of the house somehow, and onto the roof of the back porch.

A moment later she was drifting across the backyard, toward the woods. The upside-down house was growing dimmer, and she was primarily aware now of a pair of soft-clad feet moving in a steady rhythm above her head.

There were no sounds now in this dream. It was an eerily silent one—and, yes, she had defeated it.

It was pleasant, almost erotic.

Strong arms were holding her, and she had not felt so safe in years. She was no longer upside-down. She was being embraced, carried, and hugged like a precious child—and a sound of some sort had edged into the dream.

It sounded like the *thump thump thump* of a strong and steady heart.

She snuggled to that presence, clasping it in her arms and hanging on for dear life.

"Daddy," she sobbed. "Oh, Daddy!"

"It's okay," declared an incredibly soft voice beyond that heart, that incredibly strong heart. "It's okay now."

And she knew that it was true.

14: Blowing It

Domino gave the hard stare right back to the gangbusters kid as he told him, "I said you can't serve him and that's it. Mr. Sciaparelli is now in protective custody of the First U.S. District Court of New York. He has been granted full immunity against prosecution in a case now pending before that court. Any legal demands served on him in this jurisdiction could prejudice his testimony. You'll have to hold your subpoena until disposition of the New York case."

The kid wasn't backing down, though. He asked, "Are you his lawyer?"

"No. I'm an officer of the court." Domino handed over the paper work. "At Mr. Sciaparelli's own request, we are providing protective escort to New York. I'm sure you're aware of the present situation here in Atlanta. The man's life is in grave danger."

"When are you leaving?" the kid asked as he scanned the papers.

"We were just leaving when you came up."

"Sounded to me like you were just target-practicing when I came up," the Fed said cutely. "Special United States Marshals, huh. Do you mind if I check this out?"

"Suit yourself," Domino told the smartass. "Sciaparelli will probably grant you the use of his telephone."

The kid handed back the papers. He also shoved the subpoena at the Ship.

The idiot took it.

The kid said, "There's nothing here to prejudice any New York case. We've already taken the action. The service is a mere formality. Good day, Mr. Sciaparelli. I'll see you in court."

Ship took a quick step forward and blurted, "Wait, I'll go with you! Now, right now."

The kid looked at Domino—startled questions rising there, in that gaze.

A cold hand was squeezing down hard on Domino's heart. He winked at the young Fed and shook his head in a condescending manner. "He can't do that. He has a court date in New York. I'm here to see that he keeps it. Our plane is waiting."

The gangbusters kid looked at Ship. There was a whole new quality to that voice as he asked the Atlanta boss, "Do I understand that you are volunteering to accompany me to my offices? Do you wish to give a deposition?"

Perspiration was oozing down Sciaparelli's forehead. He patted at it with a handkerchief, as he replied, "That's right. I believe in meeting these things head on." He glanced nervously at Domino. "The plane can wait another hour. I don't want to leave with a lot of stuff hanging over me here."

He started moving toward the cop's car.

The guy was blowing it. More than that, he was blowing out completely. The thing was falling apart, and it was falling straight into Domino's clutching guts.

"Sciaparelli!" he barked. "Do you understand that I can't be responsible for your security if you persist in this? Do you understand that the repercussions in New York could be extremely grave?"

Ship muttered, "Yeah, yeah, I understand." He went on and got into the car.

The gangbusters kid gave Domino a shrug and a mirthless grin. "You can't win them all, Special Marshal," he said smugly.

Like hell he couldn't!

He marched to the vehicle and penetrated the defector with a knowing gaze. "It goes for Mrs. Sciaparelli," he said coldly. "She just lost her immunity, too."

The guy just sat there, looking uncomfortable.

Gangbusters nudged the Domino aside and slid in beside Sciaparelli. "Let's go," he commanded his driver.

What the hell could Domino do about it? It had caught him flat-footed and cold in the belly. The kid was still wet behind the ears, yeah, but he had a hell of a strong eye and plenty of guns to back him up. This was no place for a shoot-out with the Feds, all the goddamn dazzling front papers to hell.

He stepped back, and the car moved away.

The other cars joined the procession, and the

boss of Atlanta rolled away from there with a bona fide Federal escort.

James called over to him, "You going to let him do that?"

"Course not," Domino replied. "Send Paul. And tell Paul I don't want him coming back here alone."

James said, "Right," and moved away.

John came back from a parley beneath the portico to report: "It was Bolan, all right."

"Sure it was Bolan." The Domino was feeling sicker and sicker. "What could we do? We'd have had those gangbusters swarming all over us. You handled it right, John. Don't worry."

"The boy on the roof says he carried a woman out the back way. He's long gone by now."

"Of course he is," Domino replied calmly, belying the volcano in his belly. "What does the roof boy say about our rear guard?"

"They're all down," John reported unemotionally.

"Spider, too?"

"Spider, too. Plus two of Ship's inside boys."

The Federal procession had hit the road and was passing back westward.

Domino told his lieutenant, "I sent Paul to bring Ship back. You take some trackers to the rear. I want that boy and I want him heavy. It's twice he's made a monkey of us. It's twice he's used cops to do it. I don't like the smell. I don't like the way he always seems to know everything that's going down. I want him alive, even if it's no more than a talking head. I want that boy screaming turkey. I think we'll solve a lot of problems all over the outfit when we get that."

"Right," John said. "What do we do about the women?"

"Find Bolan, you'll find the women. Don't come back without them, John."

John said, "Right," and moved away.

Domino was left standing alone in the grass.

He could not believe it. He simply could not ...

For the first time in a long time, the headhunter felt like tearing his hair and yelling—at anything, at anybody.

Bolan! He was the guy! He was behind it *all!*

How did the goddamn guy pull such shit as that? How did he do it?

All the legends, all the stories, and the reputation of the guy had sounded like typical street-soldier romantic bullshit all this time. But now it all was like swarming bees trying to use the Domino for a hive. It was *not* just a lot of romantic ...

For the first time, Domino knew fear. Not *that* kind of fear—*that* kind of fear you lived with all the time. But for the first time in his impressive career, Domino knew the fear of failing.

How could he return to the headshed, on such a sensitive mission, without the goods?

A mild shudder traveled his full length.

To hell with *Bolan!* Bolan wasn't the *mission*— he was just an obstacle that no one could blame Domino for anyway. He wanted the guy, sure, but that was secondary.

First, he had to collect Ship and the two women.

In the process, or after the process—it mattered not—he would collect Mack Bolan's talking head.

Domino, the Blackest of all Aces, sure as hell was not going to blow this one.

He signaled to a couple of gun bearers and

made a run for his car. He was going to blow some fucking heads, that was what!

Ecclefield leaned forward across the seat as soon as they were clear of the estate and told his driver, "Turn on the CB to Channel nineteen and pass the mike back here."

The truckers' channel was very noisy. The Fed waited briefly then broke it. "This is the Screaming Eagle for a short. Is the Big Guy wearing ears?"

He was delighted and a bit surprised to receive an immediate response. "Yeah, come on back, Eagle."

"Let's Ten-twenty-seven to Seven."

"Ten-four, I'm going down."

The driver switched to Channel seven. Ecclefield announced into there, "Screaming Eagle on the break."

"Right. This one is better. I'm on you."

"How'd your thing pan out, Big Guy? I heard you coming but nothing going away."

"Right," replied that strong voice. "It went without a hitch. Love and kisses to you and all of yours. The Ten-thirty-six was perfect."

"Glad to hear it. I have a fascinating development to report."

"Is it a fit subject for citizens radio?"

"If we keep it clean, yeah. Would you believe that I came away with a male V.I.P. volunteer for room and board at my uncle's house?"

"I might believe that, yeah. Is it a V.I.P. like a ship that passes in the night?"

"That kind, yeah. You don't find that surprising?"

Bolan replied, "It sort of fits something I've

125

been looking at, Eagle. I suggest that you find him a cool room. He may be especially susceptible to heat."

"Okay, yeah, I can appreciate that."

"Also, you might look for something that came away right behind you. I'd call it that way, for sure."

"For sure, a definite Ten-four on that, okay. We'll watch it. How do you figure my roomer?"

"I'd say he's feeling a bit insecure. A lot of the V.I.P. houses are affecting people that way right now, I hear. You might talk to your fraternity brother in wonderland about that, for sure."

"For sure. I'll do that, Big Guy. I'll be close to the landline all day if you should need a Ten-twenty-one."

"Right. I'm Ten-sixty-four, down and gone."

Ecclefield sighed and passed the mike forward.

Sciaparelli growled, "What was all that shit? You think nobody knew what you were talking about?"

"Don't get testy with me, mister. I'll stop the car right here and boot you out on your own."

"You heard what your boss said. Find me a cool room."

Ecclefield found himself grinning at his prize guest. He was almost tempted to tell him who "Big Guy" really was. Almost. Not quite. If any of this afternoon's real truth should leak into the wrong ears, young David Ecclefield would need a fraternity of friends, indeed, just to keep his own ass out of the slammer.

"Cool, hell," he told the big cheese. "I'm putting you in a deep freeze, mister."

"The deeper the better, kid," Sciaparelli muttered.

"It doesn't come free, you know."

"Show me an ice cube, kid, and I'll show you any damned thing you want to know."

"Can I rely on that?"

"Long as I can rely on you, sure."

Young David could not believe his good fortune. He had something in his pocket that no one else had ever had, at any time.

He had himself a genuine singing boss. And he owed it all to the fraternity.

"Something's wrong up ahead!" his driver announced worriedly.

Ecclefield took a quick look and yelled, "Don't stop! Go around it!"

"It" was a roadblock, three automobiles wedged into an accordion formation across the narrow roadway.

And suddenly they were plunging over the curb and across the sidewalk into thick brush. There was nothing to be heard but the unceasing chatter of automatic weapons and a corresponding rain of angry hornets zipping through the vehicle, and the whole beautiful world seemed to be falling in on him.

He'd blown it, for sure.

There was nothing whatever in his pocket now but warm sticky blood and a crashing realization of failure.

A microphone was dangling just above his head. He grabbed it and punched the button to sigh, "Ten-thirty-three, Big Guy. Two minutes west of the pickup and Ten-thirty-four."

He did not know, in afterthought, why he'd done that.

Maybe he'd just wanted the big guy to know

that Young David had blown it. Maybe it was meant as a statement that the Big Guy's way was the only way. Or perhaps he'd meant it as a final farewell to the fraternity of blitzing buddies.

One did not rationalize one's own final moments.

15: Battle at Paces Ferry

Bolan's path of retreat was a little-used back road running roughly parallel to the route of the Federal convoy, and he was an estimated one mile north when he heard the Ten-thirty-three (emergency) break. His response to the help needed Ten-thirty-four was an instinctive and unthinking swerve southward, the mind pitching forward to overlay the terrain in that trouble zone in a mental search for the most likely point of ambush.

The response by the Corvette was magnificent. That super-souped power plant took the spur without a murmur of complaint to send him hurtling along that winding chute with a surge such as he had never before experienced in a land vehicle.

The center of gravity was low and the road purchase superb. Curves were something to challenge only the nerve of the driver, not the roadability of the vehicle.

And that trip was, in retrospect, somewhat akin to the launching of a rocket toward free fall in space. All the poop was delivered into the running jump; the rest was a lazy coasting. The tach needle had climbed steadily and quickly to surpass the redline and on to the peg in the first quarter-mile. He'd eased off then, fearing that the engine would blow up, and she was hovering at that redline when he executed the final curve and screamed into pay dirt. He had not noted the m.p.h. gage, only the tach, but transpired time alone told the ground-speed story.

He was at the scene in less than thirty seconds.

The lady was unconscious. She had come around briefly from the tap he'd given her, had become very emotional, and had then slipped back into the Land of Nod. She'd evidently been under severe emotional strain for quite a long time. If she felt like letting go for a while now, then the rest could only do her good—and it was good for Bolan, as well. He had not felt equipped—given the circumstances of the moment—to handle an emotionally overwrought woman.

Now, he was doubly grateful for the unconscious state of Suzy Sciaparelli. He left the car at the junction just down-range from the sounds of battle, partially concealed in bushes at the side of the road and well clear of any possibly straying bullets.

The neighborhood was a mixture of "well-fixed" and "quite well." The homes along this section of the road were irregularly spaced at intervals ranging from fifty to one hundred and fifty yards. The ambush point was at a curve and adjacent to an overgrown unimproved lot at one side of the road, with dense woods on the other.

Three vehicles with official-looking markings were forming a roadblock. A furious gun battle was in progress. Five vehicles of the Federal convoy were skewed around up-range, beyond the roadblock from Bolan's position. Apparently, he had come in on the attacker's unprotected rear.

A sixth vehicle had obviously attempted to run the blockade. It was on its side in the empty lot, bullet-riddled.

The G-men were in a bad defensive set. Three guys with choppers had cover behind the blockade. They were keeping the Feds pinned from the front while others were laying on them from the woods.

Bolan was running up on the exposed rear of the roadblock, AutoMag at the ready, when the significance of the markings on those blockade vehicles descended on him.

They were police cars.

His initial reaction to that discovery was one of horror. Was it a ghastly error in identification—with soldiers of the same side engaging one another?

Was the roadblock a police response to the gunfire on upper Paces Ferry Road?

The question was answered immediately by the evidence fresh at hand. One of the machine-gunners whirled to Bolan's approach, and Bolan immediately recognized the frozen expression of a headhunter. He'd seen the guy earlier that day at the airport.

Big Thunder boomed without considering the matter further. The guy's head exploded, splattering frothy red jelly across a police decal on the vehicle's door.

Another guy came around with his piece at full chatter. Round two ended the chatter at quarter-circle and punched the guy back the way he'd come, sending him sprawling facedown between two of the vehicles.

The third guy's attention was elsewhere. He'd risen up to duel a Fed who was advancing along the safe side of the stalled convoy. Bolan sent a pair of head busters thwacking into the base of the guy's skull in a lightning one-two, the first strike lifting him off his feet and the second tumbling him onto the hood of the vehicle.

Another guy came running out of the woods behind the block then froze in mid-stride for one startling moment of second thought, a riot gun at hip level, staring with rounded eyes at the man with the thunder-pistol. He wore the khaki uniform of a sheriff's deputy, and the face on the guy was positively ashen.

It was a rather electric situation.

Bolan had been conditioning his survival instincts since the start of this long war—conditioning them to accept death from behind a badge rather than to send death the other way.

"It's my difference," he'd kept telling himself. "It's the only definitive line between myself and the enemy."

This was admittedly a somewhat fuzzy confrontation for that instinct. It was not really a situation for instinct alone to handle. The troubling question of identity had been resolved once, at the beginning of this battle. Instinct had handled that one okay, yeah, leaping to a quick friend-or-foe identification despite the presence of confusing camouflage.

This one was different. This one involved the badge itself, and that carefully cultivated death instinct was balking at the earlier decision.

It was a moment frozen outside of time, yeah.

Instincts were obviously flowing in both directions across that moment. Either man would have been a goner for sure, otherwise.

Then the moment came unstuck and moved on.

Someone in the woods behind the deputy screamed, *"Hit'im, Billy Bob!"*

The deputy very softly said, "Fuck it." He casually showed Bolan his back and strolled nonchalantly into the covering trees.

Bolan moved off in the other direction, toward the overturned vehicle.

The gun battle beyond the barricade had taken a sudden turn for the Feds, now that the pressure was released from the front. They were getting it together now, pressing the counterattack, and the fire from the woods was becoming sporadic and disheartened.

A rear door had been thrown open at the top of the overturned car. Bolan hauled himself up there and leaned into the opening for a quick eyeball.

Two men were in there.

One was the young strike-force boss. He had blood on his head and he was twisted across the backrest of the front seat.

The other man was crumpled beneath the steering wheel.

Both were unconscious.

Bolan went quickly to work, and he had them

both lying in the grass beside the vehicle when a pair of Feds came jogging to the rescue, also.

Bolan was performing mouth-to-mouth on the driver. One of the Feds took over from him while the other examined young David.

"I think he's okay," Bolan panted. "More blood than damage. Concussion, probably."

The guy had a service .38 in his paw. He gave Bolan a long scrutiny, then sheathed the weapon.

"That was some goddamn fancy shooting, buddy," he said admiringly, "but you'd better truck it, now. I'd hate to have to explain you when the real cops show."

Bolan asked him, "Where's Sciaparelli?"

The Fed's eyes flared and leapt to the car as he replied, "Isn't he—I assumed—Ecclefield had him."

Bolan growled, "He doesn't have him now."

"Nobody came near this car, mister," the Fed said. "I had it covered all the way, ready to stop any movement on it. There wasn't any."

Bolan sighted back along the curve and told the guy, "You couldn't see the wreckage from there."

"I could see everything else."

"You couldn't see a guy moving through this grass," Bolan argued. "Maybe he crawled away. He could be hurt. I suggest you start beating these bushes."

"I suggest you truck it," the Fed replied, with a grim little smile.

Bolan curled his lips back at the guy and trucked it.

Young David would be okay, unless he could not handle a scalp laceration and mild concussion.

The rest of the strike force, except for the driver of Ecclefield's car, seemed to be okay—discounting the hurts of a couple of walking wounded who were obviously not in bad shape.

The injured driver had begun responding to the resuscitation when Bolan was relieved of the task. There were internal problems there, but he'd probably make it okay.

The only open question from the incident was the Rat of Atlanta. And, at the moment, Mack Bolan could not have possibly cared less about the fate of Charlie Sciaparelli. The guy fully deserved every unhappy thing that could possibly fall his way.

Bolan could certainly attest to that from personal observation. He had a twenty-six-year-old lady on his hands who looked forty and who may never know another totally sane day in her lifetime.

And that tragic lady's problems had not ended yet.

Another car was pulled into the bushes behind the Corvette.

Three guys were standing at Bolan's vehicle. Two were at opposite sides of the convertible, trying to drag the woman from the car, while the other merely stood and watched with a frozen face.

A familiar, frozen face. Bolan had checked out the guy earlier that day.

The Domino, yeah.

16: Living Good

Big Thunder leapt out there to hold unwaveringly on Domino's right eye from six paces out as Bolan commanded, "Leave her!"

The two guys who were leaning into the car froze at their uncomfortable positions.

A pistol was visible at Domino's belt, but the hands were a flicker too far away to try for it.

He was a cool one, though, yeah.

"This must be big bad Bolan," he said smoothly.

Big bad Bolan did not want a shoot-out—not here, not in this situation. The targets were too scattered and the woman too vulnerable to an accidental hit.

He said, "Put the lady down. We'll call it a draw. Good-bye."

"Can't do that, bad man," the ace replied. "There's no draw, and it's too tight to say good-bye. You can't take us all. So what are you going to do?"

"I'm going to start with you," Bolan told him. "Tell me good-bye or tell it to your head, guy."

"It's too dumb. We can make a deal."

"What's the deal?"

"I'll let you keep Ship. You'll let me keep the woman."

Bolan told him, "I don't have Ship, and you don't have the woman. So what's to deal?"

Bolan had been watching for it, and he got it. Those eyes. They dulled, just a whisper. The guy was losing it. He was falling apart, inside.

"Last chance to tell your head good-bye, Domino."

"Look—it's better than you think. Ship defected. He went away with some Feds. So I've lost it here. Okay. Where I've really lost it is back at the shed. You know. You and I are of the same cut. Right? Okay. All I want is a bit of dignity to take back with me. The woman will provide that. I'll settle for that now. She won't get hurt. And maybe I won't get hurt too much. It doesn't involve you at all. Why should anybody get hurt? Isn't that better than dumb?"

"She's not worth dumb, huh?"

The guys at the car were still frozen, listening with hope and maybe prayers to the debate. Both were headhunters, but not aces. All they had at stake here was life or death.

With the Domino, it was obviously much more than that.

He said, "She's not worth a damn thing to anybody—except to me. I won't leave her, Bolan. I'll say good-bye to my head first."

Bolan tried one. "She can't help you, Domino. All she knows about her father is the terror that Ship has been holding at her head all these years."

"You know about that, huh? Where the hell do you get it all, guy?"

"I live right," Bolan told him. "You don't."

Another layer fell inside the guy. The eyes receded another level inward as he replied to that. "You're wrong. You don't really have it. The only help we need from the woman is her presence in court."

"What court?"

"You know what court. And you know what's happening between the families right now. Don't you."

Bolan said, "Maybe. What's the point?"

"The point is that it's time for Ship to pay his tab. It's been called in. If I can't deliver Ship, then at least his woman is silent proof of the tab. We need it."

"Who is we?"

"You know who is we."

Yeah. Bolan knew who was we. "We" were a group of crafty old men who played curious games of deceit and intrigue while proclaiming the sanctity of brotherhood. Now, apparently, the "we" were becoming separated into factions of "us" and "them"—and some human pawn work was at hand.

Bolan said to the Black Ace, "You guys have been holding a tab for fifteen years? Come on, now."

Another layer fell. Inside, the guy was getting desperate. Neither Bolan nor Big Thunder had wavered so much as a hairline. Time was running out, and the guy knew how very little pull was left in the balance between life and death for one black ace.

He was giving it away.

"It wasn't all that important then. It's been in the bank, waiting for importance. Now it's important."

Bolan said, "Thanks, Domino. You've been everything I needed."

Then he blew the guy's dumb head off. He died without knowing that he did so.

The other two did not move or even look. They had already succumbed to combat shock.

Bolan told them, "Okay, boys, live and learn. Our deal still holds. Good-bye."

"Is it straight?" one of them croaked.

"It's straight. Beat it."

They beat it, moving swiftly to their vehicle without a backward glance.

When they pulled away, Bolan knelt beside the remains of a black ace to examine what was left there.

Yeah. This one was a real veteran—quite a bit older, really, than the new face revealed. And there was telltale evidence, at close look, of many changes of face for this guy. Probably the guy could not even recall the name he'd been born to, nor the face he'd grown to maturity with. Not even fingerprints would testify for the guy now; too many pains had been taken to insure that they would never testify against him.

Bolan sighed and placed a marksman's medal on the still chest. The mark of the beast, yeah. It was mark enough to identify this unknown soldier.

"You earned it, guy," Bolan muttered, and went to check the lady.

Her eyes were open and she was giving him a soft stare as he helped her to a comfortable position.

"Did you hear all of that?" he quietly asked her.

"Yes, I heard it," she said calmly.

"Did you understand it?"

"Yes, I understood it."

"Are you okay?"

"Sure, I'm okay. I believed you the first time. Everything is okay now."

Bolan was not so sure about that. Domino and one of his aces had gone down in the battle at Paces Ferry. But there were four aces in every deck. Two were still somewhere in play. And there was, of course, the unresolved question concerning the Rat of Atlanta.

But Bolan had no intention of burdening the lady with doubts—not now. He put the 'Vette in motion and curled an arm about her, holding her tight.

And the look in those eyes reminded him why he was smarter than a black ace.

He lived better.

17: Tracking On

The cowboy and the superskate kid had already broken camp and were preparing to make tracks when Bolan returned with his prize.

The two women fell quietly into each other's arms. Bolan sent them to the cabin and pulled the cowboy into a quiet conference.

The guy could have hardly missed the family resemblance; he knew who the lady was. "Is that what you went after?" he asked Bolan.

"That's what," Bolan said grimly.

"Must have been a hell of a squeak."

"It was that. Listen—things are coming to a head. I'm going to have to move fast if I intend to stay in front. I'll need your help."

"You've got it," the cowboy said quickly.

"Awhile ago you were telling me about an old buddy with an unforgettable name. Billy Bob."

"Yeah?"

"The guy was part of an ambush on a Federal strike force a few minutes ago. He's dirty as hell. How does that ring?"

There was no mistaking the genuineness of that surprise and mystification. "Dammit! First Shorty and now—hell, I—it's just—if you say so, okay. How do you know it was him?"

"Too much for coincidence," Bolan said. "He's a Cobb deputy and someone called his name. We were staring at each other across hot muzzles. He decided he didn't want it. He showed me his back and took a walk."

"Okay, yeah, okay. I can buy it. He's always admired you. He's got a scrapbook full of you."

"You told me he was moonlighting a job."

"Right. Some security outfit. I believe it's composed mostly of off-duty cops."

"Something's ringing here," Bolan said. "Tell me what it is."

"They guard warehouses and truck depots," the cowboy replied quietly. "How does that ring?"

"Full harmony," Bolan said. "Okay. But something is still out of quiver. I can see Domino drafting Ship's own hard forces but not his dirty cops. That doesn't fit."

"Who is Domino?"

"A headhunter from Yankeeland. Billy Bob was standing shoulder to shoulder with those people. I think I need to know what the connection is. Can you find out?"

"Watch me find out," the cowboy replied. "I'll use the phone and be right back."

"You may have to search, guy. The last I saw of your buddy, his forces were in full retreat. I'd guess they're lying low and licking wounds right now."

"I know where to search," Reynolds growled.

He went into the cabin.

Bolan checked his weapons and replenished spent clips, then he leaned against the fire-red Corvette and went to work on his diminishing energies.

When the cowboy returned minutes later, Bolan was sound asleep on his feet.

Reynolds said, "What the hell?"

Bolan's eyes cracked open. He said, "I'm here. What'd you get?"

"I got your man. He sends apologies and best wishes. Says he's turning it all in. Just trying to decide now who to turn it to."

"Give him the same guy I gave you," Bolan suggested.

"The Federal guy?"

Bolan nodded. "What's the intel?"

"Billy Bob never met the boss. He's sure it was not Sciaparelli, though. He says it was 'some people' in New York. They weren't doing security work. They were checkers."

"What were they checking?"

"Shipments."

Okay. It figured. More and more, Sciaparelli was being revealed as nothing but a front cover for the main interests up country. And they did not trust their cover. They had eyes on the guy, guarding against thievery and/or unauthorized extension of territory and power. The guy had a bit in his mouth, yeah.

"He knew about Shorty," Reynolds said.

"What'd he know?"

"He says he let it slip to Shorty a couple of months ago—Billy Bob's job with New York, I mean. He said he knew Shorty was climbing a trouble tree when he started the thing with Jennifer. Shorty had been a pretty good cop, you know. He was digging into some old stuff. Billy Bob didn't know what it was, but Shorty was going to cut him into the action as soon as he got it all sorted out. Shorty called him yesterday morning when we got back from the Detroit haul. He told Billy Bob to get it ready to start shaking the money tree—*real* money. Then last night at about nine o'clock, Billy Bob was out checking the loading at Bluebird. He said a guy named Lago and a couple other regular Bluebird security people pulled Shorty out of his cab and dragged him away. Billy Bob didn't make a move on that. He had too much of his own to cover. And he was not at all surprised when I told him that Shorty was dead."

Bolan said, "Okay. It's all coming together, now. Nine last night ties pretty close to the time when Domino was dispatched from New York. Yeah. Okay. It's making sense."

"I guess it means more to you than it does to me then."

"It will have to stay that way, cowboy, for reasons that touch neither of us directly. Well. Are you game for another game?"

"I'm just getting warmed up, guy."

Bolan grinned. "I sort of figured that. Okay. Awhile ago you were saying something about a spontaneous coffee break. How does that work?"

"You just get on the air and announce it. Before you can let go of the button, you've got a swarm."

"Truckers too?"

"Truckers especially. Particularly if the hand on the button belongs to a sweet-talking beaver. What are you working?"

"A trucker's convention," Bolan said thoughtfully. "Maybe. You know the territory better than I do. Tell me what the chances are. I want a solid embargo on all of Sciaparelli's merchandise. I may even go for a blockade—if it swings that way and if we can get some players. What do you think?"

"I guess I can get the players," the cowboy replied thoughtfully, "but I don't know how you would game-plan it."

"What's wrong with spontaneous?" Bolan asked with a cool smile.

The guy grinned back. "An embargo via Citizens Band? Hell. Why not? We do everything else on the damned thing. Why not?"

Bolan dug into his pocket and passed a small notebook to the Georgia Cowboy. "There's your list of embargoed depots. Go get your rig. It's just around the bend, buried in the bushes. I'll be guarding Channel nineteen. Let's move it quick. I want this thing going down before nightfall."

"What about the ladies?"

"I'll tuck them in. You'd better get moving."

They shook hands.

Reynolds said, "Thanks for more than you could understand, Big B."

Bolan slapped the guy on the bottom and sent him on his way.

He understood.

And it was a proud thing to see a winner stepping away from a loser's tracks.

Yeah. Bolan understood completely.

Years of constant terror could do it to a person. Bolan was well aware of that. It could be especially destructive to a soft and tender girl with strongly protective instincts—a girl such as Susan James Rossiter Sciaparelli.

Jennifer had been young enough that she "barely remembered" her father.

Susan remembered him well. And she remembered that terrible night when he'd been carried, kicking and screaming, from their modest Trenton home—never to be seen again, except in bits and pieces.

She remembered the hurried and breathless flight through the night when the other men came to bundle off the rest of the family, the quiet relocation to Georgia, the new identities, the whole strange quality of trying to adjust to a life of lies and eternal subterfuge.

Her mother had cracked early; she had never, in fact, quite recovered from that terrible night when her husband was dragged from her bed and carried away. It had been up to Susan to invent the lies for little Jennifer, to shield and protect her from the truth, to gently and carefully reprogram family memories and genealogies.

There was but one thing the mother had stood firmly against—the changing of Christian names. The girls were too old to be totally separated from their identities; the given names had stayed; the family name became Rossiter.

The physical life had been quite comfortable, from a purely financial standpoint, anyway. The monthly checks from "Daddy's insurance" were regular and generous. Special checks had always come at Christmas time and on birthdays—from "Daddy's estate."

Gradually the inevitable adjustments came and there was nothing left to remind Susan of the past except for the occasional nightmare or a violent scene in a movie or the haunted look in her mother's eyes.

Sciaparelli came into her life, in a physical sense, during her final year at college. He visited her in the dean's office and identified himself as "Santa Claus and the Birthday Bunny." He was, he explained, the executor of her father's estate.

She would be "coming into things" soon, and there were certain important details she needed to learn about a "special trust" that she was soon to come into.

The special trust, it quickly developed, was nothing other than Sciaparelli himself. They were to be married. It was not a proposal but a disposal. There was no alternative. The "gentlemen in New York" who had been protecting the James ladies all these years insisted upon it. There would be grave consequences if Susan did not cooperate. It was, after all, for the continued protection of the family. If she refused, then the gentlemen in New York could no longer take responsibility. The money would be shut off, and the gentlemen would disassociate themselves from any further participation in the family's welfare. Sciaparelli broadly hinted that each of the women would quickly share the fate of their father, once that protection had been lifted.

Everything considered, Susan James Rossiter had been a relatively happy and normal young woman of twenty-two. She had tended to shy away from serious involvement with young men—largely because of the secrets in her life—but she was immensely popular and much sought after. And she was subject to the normal expectations a young woman may have for love and marriage ... one day.

Charles Sciaparelli, a thirty-five-year-old total stranger, did not quite fit those expectations.

However, Susan was a responsible young woman—and a practical one. She accepted the situation, precisely for what it was. The new circumstances of her life were, indeed, more like the awakening from a pleasant dream to a terrible reality. She had suddenly been transported eleven years into the past with nothing changed, except that now she was a grown woman with unavoidable responsibilities.

The rest, Bolan had pretty well understood already. Jennifer had been kept ignorant of the situation while "the protections" silently wove her closer and closer into an inescapable web of confinement and entrapment. Susan had actively participated in that deception—"for Jenny's own good."

When the mother died and full responsibility descended squarely upon Susan's young shoulders, the strain slowly bore her down. She cracked, just as her mother had done—became "sickly" and a recluse, living in constant terror. What Jennifer had taken as "fascination" with regard to Susan's feelings toward her husband was, in reality, abject surrender to the inescapable realities of an impossible life.

The worse part of all, from Bolan's viewpoint, was that these girls had never been in any danger whatever. He was positive of that. It was even problematical that their father was guilty of any sin. The James women, regardless of what John Paul James may or may not have done, were innocent pawns in a wily game of move and counter-move by insanely clever old men, banked away for an incredible fifteen years against some unseeable future event for which their "tab" would be called in.

Sciaparelli had evidently been the keeper of the keys to that bank.

The guy had been in "investments" when the nightmare began for the James family. He had quickly escalated his position, perhaps parlaying some natural association with the caper into favored treatment for himself—and placing also, incidentally, his own future into that growing tab.

Whoever was providing that "bank" was not the man or men behind the attempted assassination of soon-to-be *capo* Jake Pelotti.

Huh-uh, the game did not work that way.

If the girls had been any sort of threat to the men behind the hit, they would have gone to the same fate—and at the same time—as their father.

The man or men behind the bank had to be "us," not "them."

Domino had said it well. "It wasn't all that important, then. It's been in the bank, waiting for importance. Now it's important."

Sure. The money that supported the James ladies for those fifteen incredible years had come from "us." But, bet a life on it, there would be books to show that it had come, all those years, from "them."

Incredible, sure. Nutty. Unthinkable, in a world where right made right and wrong made wrong.

Entirely credible, though, sane and very thinkable in a mirror-image world where right was dumb and wrong was smart.

Sciaparelli himself had to be, of course, party to the con. Which meant that his original sponsorship had been with "them." The guy had traded his soul for a shot at the top with "us." And now the "tab" was being called in. It was time for all players to stand up and remove their masks, reveal themselves to the nutty world of *us* and *them*.

Apparently, the dividing line between *us* and *them* was not all that stable at the moment. It rarely was. There was no clear understanding of who *us* and *them* really were; all of that depended upon the balance of power in that curious world. It was like a poker game with the deciding hand buried in what turned up in the hole cards. Identification of friend and foe could be fuzzy—just like Bolan's, back at that "police" barricade.

A savvy player like Sciaparelli would naturally be very hesitant about coming down firmly on either side of an uncertain line.

It had all come together, yeah, and Mack Bolan was sure of only one thing in the final results.

For the first time in fifteen years, the James girls were in true peril. With Sciaparelli loose and flapping, the thing could come down either way. "Them" would want the girls expunged completely. Never mind that it was all a lie. The game did not hinge upon truth and lies. The game hinged on who could prove what against whom.

On the other hand, "us" would want the girls in hand as "silent witness" for the prosecution—and

Bolan would almost as soon see them dead as in that position.

It had all come back, then, to the Sciaparelli question. And Mack Bolan had no keys left to that guy. Bolan would have to play the game as the old men played it. He would have to put pressure on the guy and hold it there until something blew. Then he would have to wipe the record clean—perfectly clean.

It was, yeah, time for a purge in Atlanta.

An Executioner's purge.

And it could not wait another hour.

18: Modulating

"Break-a-break, it's a Ten-thirty-three, and it's for all you cotton-picking super-slab jockeys. So gather round and hold the ears close. This is the Georgia Cowboy relaying a Ten-thirty-four for a guy we all admire and respect. He usually wears a black gruntsuit and packs a thundering third arm and he's always got the pedal to the metal. The one Big B is in the peaches town and you've all heard of his thing here by now. Let's have a radio silence on everything but the Ten-thirty-three and let's pack it on down to support the man. I'm going on the side for a short-short while the modulations spread, then I'll bring it on back for details on the Ten-thirty-four. Let's have it quiet and cool, cotton pickers, while the modulations ripple. This one Georgia Cowboy is on the side and looking."

"A big Ten-four on that Ten-thirty-four. How

'bout you, Big B? You got your ears on here? It's Snotty Sam on the boards and looking at you."

"Breeaak to that Georgia Cowboy and the one Big B. You've got the Arkansas Traveler looking down your Ten-thirty-four. Bring it on back here."

"Mercy goodness, it's the Florida Highroller northbound and hammer down for the Music City. But now I'm moving to the grass and looking at that Ten-thirty-four. I'm going nowhere; I'm here; come on."

"Break-a-break-a-break-break! You've got the Lovin' Spoonful looking for that big man. Got your ears on, hot rocks?"

"Clear the channel, you cotton-pickin' beaver! It's no time for goose and juice! All you silly people keep the channel clear for the Ten-thirty-three."

"Break-break, a Ten-thirty-three is going down for the big guy in Peaches Town. Spread the word on your secondary channels and keep this one clear. We standing by, we here, we the one Skater from Decatur."

"This is Atlanta Rosebud Base. We be on directional ears and beaming a standby Ten-thirty-four. All stations please stand down and keep ears tuned for the Ten-thirty-four to support the one Big B on his Atlanta bust. Rosebud Base beaming with a Ten-thirty-three . . ."

"Cotton picker nearly blew my ears off! That ain't no four-watt station!"

"Mercy, get that cotton-picking blunderbuss off the truckers' channel!"

"Break-a-break, leave the cotton picker alone. He be reaching down all the superslabs and pickin' ears all the way. Let's go Ten-twenty-three for the short-short."

"Break to that Ten-thirty-four breaker. You got the one Beaver Patrol at the malfunction junction at 285 south. We be idling here for beans and Z's, but we be wide awake now and on the side. Hurryin' Hoosier is in the pit and bringing up all the parked ears. It's the Beaver Patrol with a stationary convoy, standing by for that Ten-thirty-four."

"Break-a-break-a-break-break! It's the Georgia Cowboy again with that Ten-thirty-four. Atlanta Rosebud Base please stand by for directional rebroadcast and let's get all the ears a-listening. All you cotton-picking eighteen-wheelers with trailers to or from the following depots, the Big B requests you run naked from wherever you are and leave the cotton-picking trailers in the grass. Here we go; stand by to copy; here comes the shit list. We got the Atlanta Cooperative Association, that's ACA. We got the Georgia Perfect Brewers. We got . . ."

Bolan turned off the radio and swiped at his eyes as he returned to the cabin.

"What's wrong?" Miss Superskate asked him. "Something in your eye?"

Yeah, Bolan had something in the eye.

He had pride in the eye, and affection, and genuine respect. They were some kind of guys. There would be money lost and hauls forfeited this night—but he had no doubt whatever that the embargo would work.

He thought of David Ecclefield and his remark about "joining the fraternity."

There were fraternities and then there were fraternities.

But this one, yeah, was some damned remarkable kind of fraternity—these knights of the road.

Damn yeah.

Break-a-break yeah.

They jointly agreed on a quiet motel nearby, and Bolan saw the ladies off, in the Corvette. Then he returned to his battle cruiser and tried the mobile phone combination to strike-force headquarters.

The guy was on the job and functioning, yeah, but testy and smarting like hell.

"How's the head?" Bolan asked him.

"Better than it has a right to be," young David snapped. "I never felt so goddamn foolish in my—"

"Save that for your old age, guy," Bolan advised. "There are still many games to be played. Sure you're okay?"

"Yeah, I'm sure. But what the hell have you got going down now in this town? The whole area seems to be in a state of panic: cops are running up and down the highways like tourists; trucks are sitting around all over the goddamn place; truck stops are all jammed and in an uproar; the whole damned town is—"

"Yeah, I know," Bolan said. "Turn on your citizens radio and you'll be in the know, too. Listen to me, first. It's the most remarkable damn thing since the discovery of electricity. You cops are missing a bet if you're not making use of this phenomenon. Pretty soon, friend, you're going to see semitrailers sitting on the grass along the interstates from coast to coast and from Canada to Mexico. If somebody's smart, they'll begin an immediate movement to tag, identify, and impound those abandoned trailers. They'll find hot merchandise of one kind or another in most of them."

"Wait a minute, wait a minute. What are we talking about, in terms of sheer numbers?"

"How would I know that, David? How many truckloads does it take to make a billion bucks a year worth of hot goods?"

"Steady traffic, I guess."

"Right. You're at the heart of the action, friend, so why don't you start making like a strike force? It's all in interstate commerce; it's your jurisdiction. Maybe you should get on the hot line and cue this thing around all over. It's a plum to make Sciaparelli look like small stuff. Get those trailers while they're all in the grass, David, and you'll break the back of this operation forever. They could never absorb the loss."

The Fed was evidently mulling that one over. "How'd you turn this?" he asked quietly.

"I didn't. My road buddies turned it. It's a game called break-a-break, like in cotton-picking eighteen-wheelers and super-slab jockeys. We simply released a shit list, David."

"I don't see how that could do what you're saying. Maximum range for those radios is fifteen to twenty miles, except in extraordinary conditions. I don't see—"

"It's called a Ten-five. In this case, a spontaneous relay. It's like a chain reaction. That shit list is probably already moving along the California highways."

"That is remarkable, yeah, if true."

"I believe it's true. I know a young lady who tried it once just to experiment. The message got back to her a bit garbled in places, but she assures me it made the round trip to Los Angeles in three hours."

"I can beat the hell out of that by telephone," the Fed commented dryly.

"Sure, but you can't hit every city and hamlet along the way."

"Maybe you've got something, mister. Okay. I'll send the alert. If what you say is true, though, I shouldn't have to. The local Smokies will already be onto it. They monitor the CB, you know."

Bolan chuckled soberly and said, "Yeah, I'm counting on it. But someone may as well get official credit. Get your thing on the wire, friend. It will relieve some of the sting of your recent loss."

"I'm not in it for credits," Ecclefield replied stiffly.

Bolan said, "They help when you're going in for budget dollars, guy."

"See what you mean. There are many games to play, aren't there? I guess I'm learning."

Bolan said, "You bet you are. I'll be in touch."

He hung up and immediately put the warwagon in motion. It was time to seal the action. The pressure was bound to erupt somewhere, and soon.

And Bolan thought that he may just know where.

19: Hammer Down

The town was in an uproar, all right. Every cop in the metro area must have been on duty, and in vehicles, and patrolling the interstates and arterial surface routes. Bolan knew for a fact, also, that most of those vehicles were equipped with CB receivers and that official ears were monitoring everything that went down on the truckers' channel. He would have to safe that with all possible caution.

Decatur was a rather typical small Southern town at the eastern edge of Atlanta. The situation here was much calmer, although Bolan found the "bears" patrolling in abnormal numbers even in this area.

He found the address without difficulty and also found the beautiful old black man awaiting him at the door.

"Is it Mr. Frankie?"

"It's me, Henry. I'm looking for Sciaparelli."

The old man chuckled. "You should have been here ten minutes quicker, suh. You could have saved Henry fifty dollars."

"He was here?"

"Sho' was. Taxicab carried him. He look like the death, Mr. Frankie. Borrowed all the money I had and took the car."

"What kind of car?"

"Blue-and-white Chevrolet, but the blue has turned mostly gray. I forget the year—must be '65 or '66. Henry's getting too old to be driving, anyway. How is Miss Susan and Miss Jennifer, suh?"

"Keep the home fires burning, Henry. They'll both be coming back very soon. Miss Jennifer said to give you seventy-threes, whatever that is."

The old man beamed and said, "That girl is a sight."

"Do you have any idea where Sciaparelli was headed?"

"No, suh. He just say it's an important appointment. He look like the very death, suh. He didn't say where; he just say urgent. I guess he knew those gentlemen were chasing him."

"Which gentlemen?"

"They was going around one corner while you came around the other, suh. Two new cars just loaded down. I 'spect Henry would feel urgent, too, Mr. Frankie, with those gentlemen looking for him."

Professionals, yeah, real professionals. Those guys would not miss a trick—and it was going to be a footrace for sure, to see who would be the first to catch the guy—Bolan or the headhunters.

And it was part of the "class" of this old man to

impart the information in just that way. Bolan understood that. Henry was well aware of what was going down.

"I been listening about you on the television, Mr. Frankie." He chuckled. "They don't call you that name, of co'se."

Bolan chuckled with him. "Thanks, Henry. I appreciate the information. I meant it, about the girls. They'll be home soon."

"Thank *you*, suh."

Bolan returned to his vehicle and made tracks away from there.

He was in a furious debate with himself, in a security sense, as he rolled back through the Decatur business district, then lost the argument when he saw the city-police car parked at the main intersection.

"How 'bout that local yokel at the curb," he tried, on nineteen.

He saw the guy lean toward the mike. "Yeeeaah, what you got there, citizen?"

"You know Henry Jackson? Black man about seventy or seventy-five?"

"Sure, I know Henry. What's he done?"

"He loaned his car out and I'm trying to find it for him. Did you see it go by here?"

"About ten minutes ago, yeah. White man at the wheel. Is it hot?"

"No, it's a family friend in the car, but Henry needs it back right quick. I just thought I'd look around, for him."

"Looked like he was headed for 285. You want me to do something about it?"

"Naw, thanks. I guess you guys already got your hands full, huh?"

"Full you never heard of before, citizen. I'm Ten-twenty-three; have a good day."

The cop had been eyeballing Bolan throughout that conversation. The light changed and the war-wagon cruised on. Bolan waved at the guy as he passed. The cop waved back.

It was a small tip in a very general direction. Interstate 285 was the bypass route around the Atlanta congested area. With a ten or so minute lead, the guy could be anywhere. By now, he could be running north or south, east or west, on any of a number of wheel-spoke routes.

There was but one option for Bolan. Bears with ears or not, he had to go for broke on this one. Urgent business awaited his attention in the far north; he could dally in Dixie no longer.

As he approached the interstate, Bolan thumbed the mike and gave it a what-the-hell shout. "I need some eyes on 285."

"We got a Ten-thirty-three in progress, good buddy. Please stay off the channel."

"This is part of it," Bolan came back. "I need an eyeball on a blue-and-white Chivvy, '65 or '66 model, white male at the wheel as lone occupant, last reported out of Decatur heading toward 285."

A third guy jumped in. "Don't answer that cotton picker! He's a Smoky!"

"Negatory on that Smoky," Bolan came back. "This is the Big B, guy, and I need help. Get me an eyeball on that Chivvy."

"Mercy me. What do I do? What do you think he is?"

It was another sort of friend-or-foe dilemma. The road buddies were suspecting an entrapment. They thought that Bolan was looking for Bolan.

He hit the ramp heading north and moved into the flow of traffic. Cops were wall to wall, up here. He pulled abreast of the cab of an eighteen-wheeler and lightly tapped his horn. The trucker glanced his way. Bolan shook the mike at the guy and started talking.

"This is the Big B and I need an eyeball on the Chivvy. Please do not identify my vehicle on the air. Will you help me?"

The guy was grinning wall to wall, and the mike was in his hand at Bolan's final word. "Mercy, I just eyeballed the Big B while he talked at me, and for sure he's not in no blue-and-white Chivvy. Hey, you cotton-pickers, give the man a hand. We want an eyeball on a '65 or '66 blue-and-white Chivvy. The driver is white and male. Let's take it way out and bring it on back. Come on; we waiting; we on the side."

One of the cops to the rear must have thought he had something in sight. His gum-ball machine began flashing, and he went around Bolan with the hammer to the ground.

The trucker, now at Bolan's rear, declared, "Mercy me! Mr. Smoky done found something."

The channel was in chaos as breakers all along that circular route began relaying the eyeball request. As quickly as it began, though, the chaos ended. In the distance, faint breakers could be heard "taking it way out," but there were no strong, close-by signals to disturb local communications.

The guy behind him called up, "Good luck, Mr. B. Give 'em hell."

Bolan risked a brief, "Yeah, thanks. You too."

The guy laughed into his mike and said, "Mr. B

is an okay guy, cotton-pickers. Treat him right. Let's have that eyeball. Bring it on to the Delta Dynamo; we waiting; we on the side."

It was coming back along the other side of the circle, now. Bolan could discern through the chattering low-level interference the faintly excited report as it was passed and picked up and passed again and again.

A ten-minute lead should have meant a ten-mile separation, give or take a few. The normal CB range was about ten miles, except in difficult terrain. There, the side of a mountain could block a signal entirely. Sometimes the range was no better than a mile, less than that in unique situations. So there was no way of knowing what to expect from the gamble. But Bolan *was* expectant. And the reward was now working its way back to him. He heard it in relay, faint and far away.

"Ten-thirty-four eyeball, it's running 285 west across the Sandy Springs exit."

The guy behind him boomed in: "Did you hear that twenty, Mr. B? That's at the top of the circle. His next sharp move could be to 75 north or south."

"Ten-four and thanks," Bolan clipped back.

"He got it, cotton-pickers. The B sends a big Ten-four. Keep that eyeball working. Let's see how it runs past 75."

The thing was set in motion. Bolan would not even need to touch his transmitter again. The eyeball watch would maintain itself.

It could, of course, mean everything or nothing. It did not have to be the same vehicle. Bolan trusted the seasoned road eyes of the truckers, but blue-and-white Chevrolets were anything but rare—and, particularly in this section of the country, the older models were still very much in evidence.

And even if it were the right vehicle, those Smoky Bears out there were undoubtedly listening with great interest to the search. They would have their own eyeballs working the problem and they would be setting up a dog watch on that blue-and-white Chivvy, just waiting for the Big B to move on it.

Things were never hopeless, however. Mack Bolan had learned to quit questioning the movements of the universe. He could only play each move as it came and give his damnedest to it. He could not forethink beyond that.

But, of course, he did have access to other resources.

He consulted an automated display at his remote console to double check the local police radio frequencies, then set the scanners and threw the system on audio monitor. The console lights flickered as the scan began, and a new game was launched.

The Smokies were not the only ones with eavesdrop capability.

He told his trailing road buddy, "Bye-bye, Delta, we down, we thankful, we gone," as he put that hammer down and gave the cruiser her head.

The game was not yet lost.

20: Convoy

The chase led north, precisely back along the way he had traveled earlier to Decatur, reversing now onto I-75 and hell-bent for Marietta.

He was only about two miles south of the Marietta marker when an urgent report was passed on a police frequency, indicating that the track was leaping westward at that point. A moment later, the same "eyeball" came down on the CB channel. The police frequencies then came alive with a flurry of new instructions and reassignments. The movement was now north on U.S. 41 out of Marietta.

Bolan was feeding the automated map display for the Marietta region when a familiar sound drifted through his CB speaker, a soft and whispery modulation caressing the break. It was a female voice that sounded like candlelight and wine, silk sheets and sweet scents, and hell, there was no mistaking it.

"You big guys on I-75 make a girl feel very secure. I'm running on north toward the choo-choo city and hoping to find good company along the way. It's the Superskate Lady looking for a back door. Bring it on back, honey."

A couple of guys jumped in quick, one of them harshly scolding "that cotton-picking flaky beaver, breaking the Ten-thirty-three," but Bolan immediately recognized that one, also. It belonged to a Georgia cowboy.

"Take it down to seven, flaky breaker, if you gotta talk," the cowboy said in his concluding remarks.

Bolan quickly switched to Channel seven and made the break. "I'll talk to the lady breaker," he said. "Come on, sweetness."

"Hi, superstud. Want to back-door me on up the superslab?"

Bolan asked, "How far you going, doll?"

"As far as you'd like to go, big man. Just follow the little red car."

Bolan told her, "Just try to shake me, sexy lady."

He was both glad and mad: mad because Miss Superskate was supposed to be safely tucked away in a cool motel for the duration of hostilities; glad because the good buddies had evidently tumbled to his problem and had stepped in to lend a hand.

The police chase had been diverted onto Route 41, by one device or another. Bolan suspected that a dummy vehicle had been rung in on them. The cops would hardly divert by CB reports alone. They had methods of their own and would not be easily thrown off by bogus radio signals.

By whatever device, the cops were running off on a tangent and Bolan had been discretely advised of the true track. So, yeah, he was plenty glad.

"Do you have me in sight, big man?" asked the sultry lady.

"Negatory. What's your twenty?"

"Just passed the Marietta marker. You're going to stay with me now, aren't you?"

"Ten-four, I'm about a mile behind and closing. Do we have a convoy?"

The cowboy came in to say, "Big Ten-four on that convoy. You've got the one Shaky Jake at the front door with the hammer down. Bring it on. We got it clean and green; not a bear anywhere and nothing ahead but a ship on the horizon."

The guy was playing it nice and cool, perfectly so. He'd changed his handle to offset identification from that very warm other channel—and that "nothing but a ship" coder could mean only *the* Ship.

Bolan replied, "I got your make, Shaky Jake. It's the Happy Hunter rolling up the backside with the hammer down. Keep me advised."

"Ten-four there, Happy Hunter. I hear tell of a convoy of eighteen-wheelers rolling southbound from Dalton, and the word I get is that it meets the ship for a quick-change near the Calhoun interchange south."

"Come back on that convoy. Is that a Ten-four on eighteen-wheelers?"

"It's a big Ten-four, for sure, very definitely a southbound convoy running with heat for a rendezvous at Calhoun. They be eighteen-wheelers for sure. Ten-four?"

"What are they running, Jake?"

"They be running the warm goods, and their jockeys be Yankee-Doodlers. Ten-four?"

"Ten-four and I thank you for the info. Those jockeys be not soft but hard. Ten-four?"

"You got the big Ten-four, Hunter, on those jockeys. They be a front door and a back door with two in the rocking chair. And they be hard all the way. Shaky Jake is on the side."

Bolan put his mike down and thought about that development.

Four big diesel rigs hauling hot merchandise with armed men in the cabs?—and planning a rendezvous with Sciaparelli? Where the hell could the guy have gotten that information?

"Bring it back, Shaky Jake."

"Go."

"What's your source?"

"We be confirming through the ears at Dalton town."

"What be the source, Jake?"

The guy sounded a bit hesitant, but he brought it on. "You know the childhood buddy with the unforgettable name, Ten-Four?"

"Ten-four," Bolan replied. He sighed, thinking how curious the wheels that moved the universe.

"He be working hard since your last eyeball together. He be scratching in the sandbox and finding the roots to a dollar tree. The ship carries a lot of cargo that the ledgers never see. Ten-four?"

"Ten-four," Bolan sighed back.

"Two and two spell four, Happy Hunter. The ship is running north and the convoy south. The usual rendezvous is Calhoun. We see that ship be looking for escort to cooler places. We be putting that together."

"Ten-four," Bolan said.

Yeah. They be putting it together, all right. Damned good cops, and what a hell of a waste of talents.

"Tell the unforgettable name when you see him that the accounts are square in that big book. The Hunter would think twice about the public turn-around unless he can safe a plea and stay with the game. We got too many saviors on the crosses already. One more won't move the universe off-center, will it?"

"You just told him, Hunter. The Brown Mount is running in the rocking chair just ahead of the sexy lady."

The guy came in then with a mouthdown sound. "Thanks, big fella. I'll give it a think."

Bolan said, "Things could warm up at Calhoun. I suggest this convoy seek the cool route. Happy Hunter will run ahead and beat the bushes."

"Negatory, that is a negatory for sure!" replied the Georgia Cowboy. "The sexy lady should take the grass when we approach the marker, Ten-four on that, but that's all the cool we gonna take. This front door is movin' on with the hammer down. We clear, we gone, bye-bye."

"Brown Mount is clear, we gone, bye-bye."

And that, dammit, was that.

There was no comeback possible; nor did Bolan even desire to give one.

The sexy lady asked, "Do you have the little red car in sight?"

"Affirmative, I'm about to blow your doors off."

"Is that *you*? In *that* thing?"

"It's me."

"You'll never reach the front door in that."

He told her, "Watch me," and he gave the big Toronado power plant all the pedal there was.

He'd overtake them, sure, long before Calhoun. He'd blow their doors off, too and, if they wanted to come on along to cover the rear, then fine and dandy.

The Corvette hunched and leapt forward as he swept past in the passing lane. She began to pace him right down the track, shoulder to shoulder.

He commanded, "Lay back, lady, and get ready to hit the grass."

"That is a negatory," she replied sweetly. "We clear, we gone, b'bye."

He watched her hang up the mike and turn to him with a go-to-hell smile.

So okay.

This damn convoy, such as it was, was in a footrace to hell. It was not exactly the way Bolan would call it, but it was the way that it was.

It was too late to try changing the signals now.

And only the hands of the universe could pick up the pieces.

It all came together like a choreographer's dream. Bolan could not have called the numbers closer if he had put it on the plotting board and rehearsed beforehand.

He "blew the doors off" the Georgia Cowboy's tractor as they swept around a bend and plunged downgrade toward the Calhoun marker.

The Corvette was still shouldering him, and she had powered through the closing gap just before he overtook the cowboy, the hot little red car running up the front door in the passing lane.

Bolan caught the flash of consternation from the rig as the girl danced past.

The guy grabbed his mike and barked, "Put a rein on that hoss, lady! Bring it over! Let the man go!"

She waved without looking back, moving over in an almost lateral movement to the far right. Bolan pulled alongside and told her, "Back it down, honey. You're in the game, okay, but at least let's do it sanely. Get behind the cowboy."

She waved at that and moved behind him as he powered on by in the descent; then Bolan saw her ducking behind the diesel rig at the same instant that the play ahead materialized.

One-half mile ahead, at the bottom of the grade, an old two-tone sedan was pulling onto the median opposite four big diesel semi-trailer rigs that were stationary on the shoulder of the southbound side.

Bolan called back, "Tally ho! We go! Are you hard, back there?"

The cowboy replied, "Ten-four, we're hard!"

"I'm going for head," Bolan announced. "You guys take care of the play on the flank."

"That's a Ten-four."

A lone eighteen-wheeler that was laboring up-grade on the southbound had picked up the channel and was apparently aware of the play going down.

As Bolan flashed past in the meet, the guy called over to him, "Watch it there, good buddy. You got snakes in the grass two clicks to the rear of those eighteen-wheelers, two carloads, and they be looking mean."

The "professionals," maybe, sure—and they apparently had not missed a trick yet themselves.

Bolan told the trucker, "Thanks," and told his rear, "It could be a kicker play! Watch for snakes!"

Sure, it could be a kicker. The guys could have been playing the same game the cops were playing, all the way, except that they hadn't been suckered off at Marietta. And they could be cooling it, waiting for Bolan to show for bloody doubles.

But then he was throwing brake and making the move to the median.

He had Ship centered in his front glass as the guy opened his door and stepped to the ground.

Their eyes met for one electric instant as the guy whirled and saw what was upon him—and the tension there recalled that first meeting of the early morning when first their gazes clashed.

The guy was toting a pistol this time, and it came up in a reflex motion just before the final curtain descended upon the Rat of Atlanta.

Bolan took him with the warwagon, flattening the man down and rolling the man up as the big vehicle passed on over him.

A hard-looking guy who'd been watching the drama from ground level across the way reacted with a warning shout and a dive for cover. A pistol cracked from somewhere over there, and a slug ricocheted off the plating at Bolan's left leg.

He was extra-vehicular with the .44 thundering before the next round came from the other side— and then the cowboy and the Mountie were running up his flank with riot guns in play and holding forth.

Even above that din, Bolan heard the engine roars and screeching of tires as two heavy sedans peeled out of the bushes downrange and joined the fray in a shoulder to shoulder charge along the southbound.

The AutoMag reached out in rapid-fire to meet that charge head on at fifty yards out.

Both drivers lost control at about the same fatal instant. They swerved together in a grinding sideswipe then leapt off to either side in a quick parting.

The car in the mon ford lane hit the median, took a roll, and flipped onto it's wheels broadside across the northbound. The other one hurtled across the shoulder, climbed the embankment, and fell back onto its roof.

Bolan reloaded on the run and pumped another clip of headshrinkers into the upright vehicle on the northbound, catching them dazed and frozen in place.

One guy was still alive in there when Bolan reached the scene. He was wedged in the rear seat between two near-headless horsemen, and his eyes were the same as every man's who knows that death is here and there's no hope beyond.

"Which one are you?" Bolan asked him.

Nothing moved but the lips. "I'm John."

"That's cute," Bolan said. "Hello, John." Then he blew John away.

The other car burst into flames as Bolan jogged across the median to close on it. A half-in, half-out guy screeched a shrieking plea for help, and Bolan promptly sent him some via thunder and lightning.

Another guy had been ejected by the crash and was sprawled across the shoulder of the road, facedown and bloody.

Bolan turned him with a foot and, yeah, it was the other ace. The guy must have been dead already, but Bolan put a sealer on the guy, just for sure. He dropped a medal on him and muttered, "Hello, James or Paul. The cute is ended."

Bolan's two helpers had the other situation fully in hand. A line of tough-looking guys were lined up at one of the rigs, feet spread and hands on heads.

Bolan walked on back to the battle cruiser and beyond it.

Jennifer James was standing beside the smashed figure of Charles Sciaparelli. She shuddered and told Bolan, "Look, he died with his guns on."

"Couldn't have happened to a more deserving guy," Bolan said. He dropped a medal into the mess and led the girl to her superskate.

"It's okay now," he told her. "Go home."

"I want—where are you . . . ?"

He said, "Over the hill, pretty lady, and far away."

"Can't you—couldn't we just—just for a short-short, huh?"

He smiled, and it was a tired and regretful one he gave her as he replied, "You need some new theories, honey. Get to work on that, huh?"

Those great eyes dropped. She said, "It's just a game, anyway. What's so important about the theories, huh?"

The big tired guy's gaze swept that tortured landscape of the Dixie Corridor and the human litter once again deposited there as he suggested to the overprotected young lady, "Ask Susan."

He left her standing there with nothing at all to hold her to discarded theories.

A moment later he was in the warwagon and

pulling out for the northbound roll toward another desecrated ground.

The cowboy noted the departure and quickly climbed into one of the captured rigs. A moment later, Bolan heard the guy's farewell.

"We thank you for the visit, big man. Come and see us again when we're all looking better."

Bolan replied, "I never saw anything more beautiful than right now," and meant it. "It's a bonny night for trucking, though, and it's time to clear this Ten-thirty-four. Please pass my appreciation. And keep the hammer down, guy."

"Y'all come back, now," invited a whispery siren of the superslabs.

And Bolan hoped that he would.

Some day, yeah, Bolan hoped that he could.

Epilogue

He tried a mobile phone combination from Chattanooga and caught the man as he was going out the door.

"How is the citizen's blockade going?" he asked the Fed.

"Looks like you were partly right, anyway," Ecclefield reported soberly. "It's working in this area, for sure. Haven't you seen?"

Bolan replied, "I'm long gone, friend, but yeah, I've seen a few trailers in the grass here and there. Work it to a proper conclusion, guy."

"You know I will. And—listen, friend, if you ever need a friend again . . . pull the chain."

Bolan chuckled and told the guy, "I'll call you, don't call me."

"Hell, don't worry," the Fed said. "I got enough games of my own."

"Right," Bolan said quietly and struck the combination.

Games enough ahead for everyone, sure.

And Mack Bolan knew, at that moment, that he was right now headed for the grimmest game of all.

Pittsfield was next on tap.

the Executioner

The gutsiest, most exciting hero in years. Imagine a guy at war with the Godfather and all his Mafioso relatives! He's rough, he's deadly, he's a law unto himself — nothing and nobody stops him!

THE EXECUTIONER SERIES by DON PENDLETON

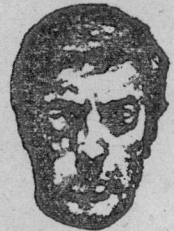

THE INCREDIBLE ACTION PACKED SERIES

DEATH MERCHANT

by Joseph Rosenberger

His name is Richard Camellion, he's a master of disguise, deception and destruction. He does what the CIA and FBI cannot do.

Order		Title	Book #	Price
_____	# 1	THE DEATH MERCHANT	P211	$ .95
_____	# 2	OPERATION OVERKILL	P245	$ .95
_____	# 3	THE PSYCHOTRON PLOT	P117	$ .95
_____	# 4	CHINESE CONSPIRACY	P168	$ .95
_____	# 5	SATAN STRIKE	P182	$ .95
_____	# 6	ALBANIAN CONNECTION	P670	$1.25
_____	# 7	CASTRO FILE	P264	$ .95
_____	# 8	BILLIONAIRE MISSION	P339	$ .95
_____	# 9	THE LASER WAR	P399	$ .95
_____	#10	THE MAINLINE PLOT	P473	$1.25
_____	#11	MANHATTAN WIPEOUT	P561	$1.25
_____	#12	THE KGB FRAME	P642	$1.25
_____	#13	THE MATO GROSSO HORROR	P705	$1.25
_____	#14	VENGEANCE OF THE GOLDEN HAWK	P796	$1.25
_____	#15	THE IRON SWASTIKA PLOT	P823	$1.25
_____	#16	INVASION OF THE CLONES	P857	$1.25
_____	#17	THE ZEMLYA EXPEDITION	P880	$1.25

TO ORDER

Please check the space next to the book/s you want, send this order form together with your check or money order, include the price of the book/s and 25¢ for handling and mailing to:
PINNACLE BOOKS, INC. / P.O. BOX 4347
Grand Central Station / New York, N.Y. 10017

☐ CHECK HERE IF YOU WANT A FREE CATALOG

I have enclosed $_____ check_____ or money order_____
as payment in full. No C.O.D.'s.

Name_____

Address_____

City_____ State_____ Zip_____
(Please allow time for delivery.)   PB-36